THE BLAZING LIGHTS OF THE SUN

Rosita Copioli

THE BLAZING LIGHTS OF THE SUN

A BILINGUAL EDITION

*Translated from the Italian by
Renata Treitel*

LOS ANGELES
SUN & MOON PRESS
1996

Sun & Moon Press
A Program of The Contemporary Arts Educational Project, Inc.
a nonprofit corporation
6026 Wilshire Boulevard, Los Angeles, California 90036

This book first published in paperback in 1996 by Sun & Moon Press
10 9 8 7 6 5 4 3 2 1
FIRST EDITION
English language translation ©1996 by Renata Treitel
©1979 by Rosita Copioli
Published in Italian as *Splendida lumina solis*
(Forlì: Forum / Quinta Generazione, 1979)
Reprinted by permission of the author.
Biographical material ©1996 by Sun & Moon Press
All rights reserved

This book was made possible, in part, through contributions to
The Contemporary Arts Educational Project, Inc.,
a nonprofit corporation

Some of these poems previously appeared in English in
International Poetry Review, Kestrel, Paintbrush, Poetry New York and
The Snail's Pace Review. The translator would like to thank
the editors of these publications.

Cover: Theo von Doesburg, *Cosmic Sun*, 1915
Design: Katie Messborn
Typography: Guy Bennett

LIBRARY OF CONGRESS CATALOGING IN PUBLICATION DATA
Copioli, Rosita [1948]
The Blazing Lights of the Sun
p. cm — (Sun & Moon Classics: 84)
ISBN: 1-55713-195-3
I. Title. II. Series.
811'.54—dc20

Printed in the United States of America on acid-free paper.

Without limiting the rights under copyright reserved here,
no part of this publication may be reproduced, stored in or introduced into
a retrieval system, or transmitted, in any form or by any means
(electronic, mechanical, photocopying, recording or otherwise),
without the prior written permission of both the copyright owner
and the above publisher of the book.

Contents

Translator's Note 9
Acknowledgments 13
Preface by Giuseppe Conte 15
Il riposo del verde 20
    The Repose of the Green 21
Narciso 22
    Narcissus 23
Penteo 24
    Pentheus 25
Daphne 26
    Daphne 27
Flora 28
    Flora 29
Muscosi fontes 30
    "*Mossy springs, and grass...*" 31
Per Virgilio 32
    For Virgil 33
Bianco 36
    White 37
Albero 38
    Tree 39
Marina 40
    Marina 41

Il viola non è un colore 44
   Violet Is Not a Color 45
Gypsophila 46
   Gypsophila 47
A Campana 48
   To Campana 48
Chi 50
   Who 51
L'anima del vegetale 52
   The Vegetative Soul 53
Una sorte 56
   A Fortune 57
In conclusione 58
   In Conclusion 59
Resta il confine 62
   "The boundary remains…" 63
Di quale nitido stupore 64
   "You bow with such neat astonishment…" 65
Trionfo di me, mi affondo 66
   "I triumph…" 67
Saggio fisico dell'instabilità 70
   Physical Test of Instability 71
Luce 72
   "Light of a clear light…" 73
Di una benevola oblivione 74
   "Let us scan proof upon proof…" 75
Fiori per te, nel tuo anniversario 76
   Flowers for You, on Your Anniversary 77
Il tempo è dolce 78
   "The weather is fair…" 79

Guarda, tutto ritorna   80
    "Look, everything returns..."   81
Quae nemora   84
    "What groves, what glades..."   85
Come le nature morte   90
    "Like still lifes..."   91
Denique   92
    "Again,..."   93
Vides   98
    "You see..."   99
Giallo la curva molle del vetro   100
    "Yellow, the soft curve of the yellow..."   101
Suavis tempestas   104
    Suavis Tempestas   105
E se, favoleggiando gli antichi   114
    "And if, when the ancients..."   115
Author's Note   120/121

Notes   123

Translator's Note

Beauty is the main reason to engage in a translation. Beauty of language, beauty of voice, beauty of vision. In the case of Ms. Copioli, a first reading of *Splendida lumina solis* convinced this translator that here was an important and wonderful new poet who filled the gap between the Italian poets of the 1960s, the so-called *I novissimi*, and the later generation of writers.

The Italian poets belonging to the generation of the 1960s, truly a new avant-garde group—Giuliani, Porta, Sanguineti, Spatola, Balestrini, to mention a few—aimed at causing "shock and provocation." To do so, they used the "specific means of...discontinuity of the imaginative process, lack of traditional syntax, and...violence of images."* They also engaged the reader in the act of creation by making him/her an active participant in the reading process itself. They are all concerned with the loss of meaning in modern language and the loss of meaning in modern life. Existentialism, phenomenology and all of the philosophical concerns of the twentieth century influenced their writ-

---

* *The New Italian Poetry. 1945 to the Present. A Bilingual Anthology.* Edited and Translated by Lawrence R. Smith. Berkeley, University of California Press. 1981. pp. 30–31.

ing subtly undermining the content of their poetry. Indirectly, they influenced Ms. Copioli.

A pupil of Luciano Anceschi, under whom she studied Aesthetics at the University of Bologna, editor of *L'altro versante*, a journal of poetry and criticism, author of two collections of poetry and two volumes of essays, Ms. Copioli is comfortable with the classics as well as with the Italian, European and American literatures. Her education in the decade of the 1960s grounded her in the many critical theories of our times. So it is not surprising that she writes poetry that belongs to her age and yet is fiercely her own—no easy fashions or trends for Ms. Copioli—poetry that is both contemporary and timeless and where the great writers of the Western civilization speak: from Pindar to Lucretius, to Ovid, to Dante, to Leopardi, to Yeats, to T.S. Eliot, to Verlaine, to Marianne Moore and others, but also where the philosophical concerns of her generation are present.

Unlike E. Sanguineti, who uses the contaminated Latin of the late Roman writers in a parodic way, Ms. Copioli appropriates lines from the traditional classical writers and weaves them verbatim or with minor changes, to suit her needs, into her own text. Though she gives references, she does so inconsistently and in a general way. For instance, she tells the reader to keep in mind the spirit of a certain book of Lucretius' *De rerum natura*, but she uses only one line from that particular book. Sometimes she quotes line numbers but other times she does not do so. She weaves these Latin lines into her own text without any typographical change, so that the reader moves from Italian to Latin and back to Italian according to Ms. Copioli's poetical muse.

Like Lucretius, Ms. Copioli is concerned with life: its source, its goal, its mystery. Like Leopardi, the great Italian Romantic poet, she is concerned with the concept of the infinite. Like Yeats, she is concerned with myth. Thus, she returns to the idea of nature as metamorphosis, to the idea of a primeval botany, to a prehistoric vegetable life prior to animals and man, to the emergence of a non-human world of births and rebirths. In many ways, *Splendida lumina solis* is a genesis, a female genesis, reflecting a myth of origin as an expression of the chaos which precedes and justifies cosmic order and reflecting a vision of female auto-erotic fantasies of generation without copulation. From the succinctness of the first poems in *Splendida lumina solis* to the luxuriant and absolutely out-of-bounds last poem, for which the horizontal line is not enough anymore, Ms. Copioli's text gives physicality to the world of origins and growth: from the seemingly lifeless winter plant to the exuberance, vigor, lusciousness of a nature which "grows of its own accord."

What makes *Splendida lumina solis* such a fascinating work is not only Ms. Copioli's link both to the classical tradition and to the philosophical theories of the twentieth century, but also the fact that in a second collection published in 1989, *Il furore delle rose,* her style departs from the difficult, laborious, fragmented and yet passionate style of the present collection.

When the translation of *Splendida lumina solis* was first completed as part of a project sponsored by the The Witter Bynner Foundation for Poetry, this translator's impulse—maximum fidelity to the original—was to translate the text into English keeping the Latin lines as they appear in the

Italian collection. Translation of the Latin was given in English as a footnote at the bottom of each page.

However, on preparing this volume for publication, it was pointed out to this translator how the movement of the reader's eye to the English footnote stopped the flow of the reading. Since a smooth reading was of paramount importance and absolutely indispensable if the reader was to experience the deep passion of Ms. Copioli's poetry, the decision was made to place all Latin quotes as endnotes while incorporating the English into the main body of the translation. One concession was made to the original: the English substitutions are printed in italics.

Ms. Copioli borrows mainly from three authors: Ovid's *Metamorphoses*, Lucretius' *De rerum natura* and Virgil's *Eclogues* and *The Aeneid*. At first, Beatrice Notley assisted with the Latin part of this translation. However, when the decision was made to keep the text totally in English, this translator began searching for the work done by other translators and, in particular, for poetry translations of the classics. The result is shown in the bibliography at the end of the book. Furthermore, the name of the translator appears in parenthesis next to each Latin footnote. The name of several translators is given in parenthesis when the English borrows from various versions. Where no source for the Latin was found, the English is based on Ms. Notley's version.

Hopefully, the passion and beauty of Ms. Copioli's poetry is preserved and the reader will enjoy the text for itself and for the many reverberations across the centuries.

—RENATA TREITEL

Acknowledgments

My grateful thanks to the Witter Bynner Foundation for Poetry, Inc., for a grant which provided support and encouragement during the completion of this manuscript.

My friend, Margherita Guidacci, well-known Italian poet and translator, for bringing to my attention the work of Rosita Copioli.

Beatrice Notley, for her indispensable, detailed translation of all Latin quotes in the early stages of this translation project, when neither the Italian nor the Latin were readily understandable.

The library at the University of Tulsa and the Tulsa-County Public Library for invaluable help from their Readers' Reference Service. And Thomas Benedictson, at the University of Tulsa, for help with the Greek in the poem "*Let us scan proof upon proof...*"

Rina Ferrarelli, published poet and translator, gave my manuscript a close bilingual reading. She was instrumental in my decision to change the format of the original by placing all Latin quotes as endnotes, while incorporating the English equivalents into the main body of the translation. Ms. Ferrarelli also suggested the use of a "well-known published translation [of the Classics] giving the translator credit." The manuscript has gained in fluidity and the reading comes closer to Ms. Copioli's intentions. To her go my special thanks and deepest gratitude.

Rosita Copioli who, over the years—both by mail and in person in Rimini, Italy—answered the many questions raised by her work.

Kathy McCullough, Sue Bishop, Nancy Davis, and Cheryl Gravis, poets in their own right, for a critical reading of the English at different stages of the translation.

Finally, my gratitude also to all the poets and translators whose work paved the way for me and whose presence, literally and figuratively, made my road less solitary.

Preface

I have often thought of poetry as a prehistoric dream: a dream born before the unity of conscience, of family, of state, of monotheism; a dream born before language and which, nevertheless, had to wait for language in order to become incarnate and be kindled by a fire that has never stopped. Language is an instrument of separation, of classification, of knowledge. The prehistoric dream of poetry instead gives back to language the functions of totality, of chaos, of intoxication: impossible functions, to be sure, *dreamed in the form*. Little by little, language has given in to the needs of history, of civilization, of idealogy, and little by little, poetry has kept that primeval fire burning and has branded man with his throbbing continuity with nature, his indomitable request for joy, his fluid desire for metamorphoses.

All of this has always taken shape within the Space of a Form—magnificent, costly, intransitive, useless—within a Figure, within an Institution.

Therefore the labor of poetry has essentially oxymoronic statutes: it takes shape within history and within language, but it has always to deal with the prehistoric and the nonlinguistic: when the labor is successful, it carves out spaces of splendor inside language and finds the being under the diachronic; like the wind which whips the thick, grey, compact branches of the eucalyptus, opening blue gaps in them, and shakes them all the way to their well-rooted, motionless trunks.

Different from the new poetry which has recently appeared in Italy, Rosita Copioli has relied on poetical premises not unlike the ones mentioned above. Yet, no matter how solitary and unfathomable, her experience also takes us back to that new poetry. I would like to point out from the beginning, and without the wisdom of a hearsay report but with the violence of enthusiasm, Ms. Copioli's inaugural botany, its vegetable prehistory: among her flowers, the dill, the Equisetum—both the archaic and the alluvial—and the freesias and the morning glories, the latter more domestic but no less secret (the late morning glory is born a few days before the winter solstice, its deep-blue color now faint lilac, its size dwarfed compared to the August blooms, with no substance to oppose the wind). Ms. Copioli seems to be drawn to this life of metamorphoses, of decay and of dazzling flashes. Her longer poem "And if, when the ancients were telling tales," elicits our love for its energy of movement, for its tracing the emergence of a non-human world of births and rebirths, for its feeling of a *diffused divinity*. It is a text about absolute, spasmodic, non-Western, "outside"-man stance, about the life of trees and flowers, not seen in a symbolic dimension, but pushed backwards in time to their original sense of life forces, in a cosmogonic dimension which, unavoidably, makes us think of the world of D.H. Lawrence.

In Rosita Copioli's poetry, myth is restored to its tale-telling function in which Latin occurs as a metamorphic, estranging, joyful, though not parodic sign (and hers is not even the late, contaminated Latin favored by Sanguineti; it is the undulating Latin of the classical dream). Next, there is a mythical *rhythm*. While in the longer poems, like "*Suavis tempestas,*" "And if, when the ancients were telling tales," "*What groves, what glades…,*" the line seems lengthened by the relentless pressing of a syntax freely renovated from the brief dimension of the shorter poems like "Pentheus," "Flora," and "The Repose of the Green," the line scans according to a rhythm that is nimble, distant, magic before arriving to metrical solutions ("You bow with such neat astonishment and at / a distance of evenings you unfold again a spirit…") of a spell-binding presence, both light and sensuous, which takes us back across a few decades to remind us, perhaps, of *Acque e Terre*,* but like a necessary, accurate remake today.

I do not know anything about Rosita Copioli except what I read in her poems: and in her poems there is hardly any trace of the biographical. However, there are some poems like "Flowers for You, on Your Anniversary," "The weather is fair, but not to quiver is an unravelling of all yesses," "Look, everything returns, even the signs on the wall" which I recommend for their sumptuously and gently metaphoric body both spacious and utterable. There surfaces in them a kind of tumultuous, but also rare and new, love for the living, which tells us what we need to know about Ms. Copioli, which is truly *engaging*: set in motion by an un-

---

* By Salvatore Quasimodo (1901–1969), Italian poet.

fathomable desire, Rosita Copioli has been able to evade the traps of metalanguage, of idealogy, of the Oedipal triangle, and of the technology of the unconscious. She has been able to place herself at the point where one meets polytheism: and has had the unbearable courage, to be docile with the sun:

> ...I shine with sun
> and the sun lends me the will.

Finally, the main requirement for writing a book such as the present one is that the book have its own *light*.

—GIUSEPPE CONTE
Translated by R. T.

*These [atoms] provide thin air,
even the blazing lights of the sun are enough for us*[1]
  LUCRETIUS,
   De rerum natura, L. II VV. 107–108

IL RIPOSO DEL VERDE

Edere erranti, dove elicrisio giacente
senza forza trarrà i profumi dove una
situazione sospesa, dal grappolo del bambino
lasciato a sé, dall'acero verde non ancora in foglie,
da una sete del corilo ingemmato,
da una verde campana d'acqua, di gemme d'acqua e
di foglie si scioglierà il riposo di tutti
il riposo del verde.

THE REPOSE OF THE GREEN

Wandering ivies, where helichrysum[1] reclines
strengthless drawing forth perfumes where a
suspended state, from the bunch of the child
left to himself, from the green maple not yet in leaf,
from the thirst of the hazelnut in bud,
from a green bell of water, of buds of water and
leaves, the repose of all the repose of the green
will unfold.

NARCISO

Diamo del paesaggio la curva che pende—
        file di ciliegi—filari—
          e àriston men ùdor, dove svelta
    si scioglie, guizza senza fatica, vien su
    dove arrides—le lacrime che notai in me
    eran tue—lacrimante—
    e così / come la cera bionda—
    né il vigore e le forze—
    si scioglie al sole tiepido—
Sic attenuatus amore / liquitur et tecto paulatim carpitur igni—

NARCISSUS

Let us give the leaning curve of the landscape—
      rows and rows of cherry trees—
        and *the water is excellent,*[1] where swiftly
it melts, darts with no effort, bubbles up
where *you smile,*—[2] the tears I noticed in myself
were yours—o tearful one—
and thus / like the yellow wax—
with no vigor with no strength—
he melts in the lukewarm sun—
So in the hidden fire of passion, he wanes slowly—[3]

PENTEO

Per me, Penteo uscito dal coro—
cacciato dal mondo—fuori e dentro le rocce—
valica discese, scendi i colli del muschio—
afferra l'albaspina—
odora le spirali del tempo.

Né bipenne d'argento, né la grazia
della caccia, né tronchi
sepolti, né gocciolare di
onde, né corna di luna—
né mani né acque, né siepi né dardi,
                Penteo.

Accessi sacris, Baccheaque sacra frequento.

PENTHEUS

For me, Pentheus left the chorus—
driven from the world—in and out of cliffs—
stride slopes, descend the mossy hills—
grab the hawthorn—
smell the spirals of time.

Neither the silver twin-bladed axe, nor the grace
of the hunt, nor buried
tree trunks, nor the dripping of
waves, nor the horns of the moon—
neither hands nor waters, neither hedges nor darts,
          Pentheus.

I found my way to the rites of Bacchus, and I still continue
    [to be his devotee.[1]

DAPHNE

Mollia cinguntur tenui praecordia libro,
In frondem crines, in ramos brachia crescunt;
Pes modo tam velox pigris radicibus haeret—

Un grave torpore occupa le membra, e
a lei il dio/ ———

ti snida, inseguita, ed ecco le tracce, tu in fuga,
le macchie, il cielo oscurato,
le fronde,—fitte sul fiume—   e
foglie di quale giardino —
      —oscurità profumata—
   —Sponda di Arnheim—
Continua il sole a cercare
      mentre
   praedam pedibus petit,
si schiarano le foglie buie—
   Apollo divampa—
pur bui i rami si chiudono, pur neri
   si chiamano bui profumi,
      —pur neri—
      Daphne

DAPHNE

When her limbs grow numb and heavy, her soft breasts
are closed with delicate bark, her hair are leaves, her arms branches,
and her speedy feet rooted and held,...[1]

A heavy numbness invades her limbs, and
to her the god / ———

he rouses you, pursues you, and now the tracks, you fleeing,
the thickets, the dim sky,
the fronds,—dense on the river—   and
leaves of what garden—
      —perfumed darkness—
   —Shores of Arnheim—
The sun keeps searching
      while
  Apollo came following fast[2]
the dark leaves grow brighter—
   Apollo blazes forth—
though dark the branches close, though black
   the dark perfumes call one another,
      —though black—
   Daphne.

FLORA

Mansit odor
            allora
nell'aria tiepida
            tenues secessit in auras.
Scrollando i capelli
            e non solo così
            posses scire fuisse deam—
Sollevata l'aria dai fiori—
mentre sostavano le luci—
o poiché rilucono i campi
di fiori purpurei,
nessun altro colore
l'aria tratteneva—
Porpora
            (porpora)
e se è possibile
fiori di porpora—
            o Flora.

FLORA

The scents remained [1]
> then
in the warm air
> *she drew near in the soft breeze.*[2]
Shaking her hair
> and not only by this
> *you could have known she was a goddess—*[3]
The air rose from the flowers—
while the lights lingered—
or since the fields are resplendent
with purple flowers,
the air held
no other color—
Purple
> (purple)
and if it's possible
flowers of purple—
> o Flora.

Muscosi fontes et somno mollior herba,
et quae vos rara viridis tegit arbutus umbra,
solstitium pecori defendite: iam venit aestas
torrida, iam lento turgent in palmite gemmae.

>   Et somno mollior herba.
>   l'erba più molle
>   ma dell'erba più molle il sonno che
>   copre gli occhi stanchi, e aspetta all'ultima
>   ora i sogni dei sogni, per gettarsi sull'erba
>   molle, che voi rara viridis tegit arbutus umbra
>   e già gli occhi stanchi, nell'ozio lungo
>   del sonno, dal mattutino albore sospinti,
>   guardano le rughe del muro,
>   leggono difese del sole su terrazze a picco.
>   E' certo che vien l'estate
>   torrida, iam lento turgent in palmite gemmae,
>   e così sotto le piante un nuovo piacere
>   mattutino e serale sarà per gli occhi
>   e i sogni, gettati sull'erba molle
>   nell'anticipo lento, nel fuggire precoce,
>   dell'estate che va.

Mossy springs, and grass softer than sleep,
and green arbutus that shields you with its scant shade,
ward the noontide heat from my flock. Now comes the summer's
parching, now the buds swell on the gladsome tendril.[1]

> *And grass softer than sleep*[2]
> the softest grass
> but softer than grass is sleep, which
> covers the drowsy eyes and waits to the very
> end for the dreams of dreams to fling itself on the soft
> grass, *green arbutus shields you with its scant shade*[3]
> and already the drowsy eyes, driven by dawn's light into
> the long leisure of sleep,
> stare at the wrinkles on the wall,
> read the sun's defenses on vertical terraces.
> It is certain, the torrid
> summer is coming, *now the buds swell on the gladsome tendril,*[4]
> and thus, under the plants, there will be a new
> morning and evening pleasure for the eyes and the
> dreams scattered on the soft grass
> in the slow anticipation, in the precocious flight
> of the summer that unfolds.

PER VIRGILIO

Un bucolico seme è già nato;
    mentre si pregano i fanciulli
    che fuggano.
(Raccolgono fiori et humi nascentia fraga).
Come dare e non dare le immagini—
le ombre (dell'incertezza)…
l'antro che silvestris raris sparsit labrusca racemis,
mentre ti chiamano i bambini—
si pregano che fuggano—
—immagini che—
chi le vuole trattare…
costano—quanto—
ozio concesso—ozio contrabbandato
che non si può
        che non si accetta—
adspice—
    scrivi all'indietro—
        torna se puoi—racconta—
importa per chi?
sive sub incertas zephyris motantibus umbras,
da dare a chi—
        le immagini—
e non più disposti a pesarle né vederle;

FOR VIRGIL

A bucolic seed is already born;
    while you beg the children
    to run away.
(They gather flowers *and low-growing strawberries*[1]).
How can one give and not give the images—
the shadows (of uncertainty)…
the cave which *the wild vine sprinkles with its stray clusters,*[2]
while the children call you—
you beg them to run away—
—images which—
whoever wants to discuss them…
cost—how much—
idleness granted—idleness smuggled in
one cannot—
        one does not accept—
look![3]—
    write backwards—
        go back if you can—tell—
does it matter for whom?
whether we pass beneath the shades that shift when Zephyrus stirs [4]
to give to whom—
    the images—
and no longer willing to weigh or to see them;

si sa piuttosto se
possono ancora andare?
Vanno ancora?
    Neppure svendute,
        e il prezzo?
Lenta salix quantum pallenti cedit olivae,
puniceis humilis quantum saliunca rosetis...
Repertori, elenchi, numerazioni—
    elenchi a non finire.
Daphnis ego in silvis, hinc usque ad sidera notus...
elenchi di nomi in arbusti e di erbe
in selve di selve,
elenchi (ancora):
là dove cadono
    altis de montibus umbrae.

does anyone know whether
they can still go?
Do they still go?
    Not even undersold,
        and the price?
As much as the lithe willow yields to the pale olive,
by as much the lowly nard yields to the crimson rosebeds...[5]
Lists, directories, numbers
    never-ending directories.
I am Daphnis amid the woods, known from here even to the stars...[6]
directories of names in shrubs and of grasses
in forests of forests,
directories (again):
there where shadows fall
        from the mountain-heights.[7]

BIANCO

Schierato viale di frutti albente di vento va a soffiare
corolle a mezz'aria, i fasci tra cielo e terra di brume e
rari oggetti, i petali che precipita la sera.
      Le rame, le brume
dai ventri del legno i già frutti—piano del bianco dolce
fluire dei petali scossi.
Schierati i ciliegi le sere, che precipita il buio le
      fisionomie dei rari oggetti
si tiene, inefficace l'abbraccio del vento e
il crepuscolo rotto dal fiore maturo
si sfa sui fili dell'erba.

WHITE

Fruit tree lined avenue albescent with corollas
wind-blown in midair, beams of mists and rare objects
between sky and earth, petals that evening flings down.
        Limbs, mists
from the bellies of the wood already fruit—plane of the white soft
drift of fluttering petals.
Cherry trees lined up in the evenings, when darkness flings down
        the outlines of the rare objects,
when the embrace of the wind holds weakly and
sunset, broken by the ripe blossom,
unravels on the leaves of grass.

ALBERO

Parlare, se parlare degli alberi è parlare di te
parlare, vedere e sapere, se parlare e vedere
è sapere che gli alberi sono ancora quelli dai nomi fioriti
che dentro le strade se ne può vedere la fine
e giardini di segni e di lunghi ciuffi rotanti
scompongono l'immagine del nostro giardino.
Che dietro ogni segno rimane l'immagine
dell'albero, quello che né un medioevo di paradisi
né alcun giardino incantato ha voluto; pianta
che in sé solo sé si nasconde e apprezza solo
                         il suo fiorire legnoso.
Uno sdegno incalcolabile ha saputo parlare
                         dell'albero
di quest'albero che è
che non sfugge, e si vede e ne parla chi vuole
e si vede e si sa.
L'albero che è e lo sdegno non tocca,
che non è sul brillante sentiero dell'Eden.

TREE

To speak, if to speak of trees is to speak of you
to speak, to see and to know, if to speak and see
is to know that the trees are still the ones with the flowery names
that their end can be seen down the roads
and gardens of signs and rotating tall tufts
ruffle the image of our garden.
That behind every sign remains the image
of the tree, the one which neither a Middle Ages of paradises
nor any enchanted garden has ever wanted; a plant
which in itself hides only itself and values only
                            its woody flowering.
An unfathomable disdain knew how to speak
                   of the tree
of this tree which is
which does not flee, and one can see and speak of it
and one sees and knows it.
The tree which is and whom disdain cannot touch,
which is not on the bright path of Eden.

MARINA

La costa s'inarca
      e
      su midolla di sabbia una falda grava s'inarca
      protende
      sue lingue sottili un
            fluido cristallo
      protende le lingue
            sottili la spiaggia
                protesa
      s'inarca nella
        dilatazione
        dell'acqua.
Schiume barbe di alabastri di
    crespe e di
        schiume sopr'acqua
        liscie e fluide crespe e lingue
          fluide
alabastrini cristalli e   barbe e lingue
      fluidi   fluide
      schiuma sottile
      protende.
Midolla di sabbia grave
        s'inarca la proda

MARINA

The seashore arches
        and
      on sandy marrow the shallow sinks, arches,
    stretches out
    its slender tongues a
        fluid crystal
    stretches out the tongues
        slender the beach
                stretched out
    arches in the
      expanse
      of the water.
Foams, plumes of alabaster, of
    crests and of
      foams above water
      smooth and fluid crests and tongues
      fluid
alabaster crystals and   plumes and tongues
      fluid   fluid
      slender foam
      stretches out.
Marrow of sunken sand
      the shore arches

                    la falda
             protende
velluti
             d'acqua di sabbia
             velluti
spenti sott'acqua
nel fondo
             tentazioni nel
             fondo velluto.
Cedevole e molle il fondo
             il piede e la mano conchiusi
tentanti gli apre e dietro
             dietro l'acqua si apre
             l'acqua dietro s'inarca
come   la falda
come   la proda
             uno specchio
il sogno s'inarca
si chiude molle la sabbia
             nel sogno
             molle si veste
riapre alla mano
             si cede si schiude
premuta
cedevole al sogno
che
penetra il sogno nel fondo.

            the shallow
        stretches out
velvets
        of water of sand
        velvets
spent under water
at the bottom
        temptations at the
        bottom velvet.
Yielding and soft the bottom
        opens the groping
clasped foot and hand and behind
        behind the water opens
        the water behind arches
like   the shallow
like   the shore
        a mirror
the dream arches
the sand closes softly
        in the dream
        softly the sand covers itself
opens again to the hand
        yields and opens
pressed
yielding to the dream
which
pierces the dream at the bottom.

IL VIOLA NON È UN COLORE

Viola delle siringhe e lenta
        come le spiree delle onde ricurve
lente come il viola le siringhe
        cadono disuguali.
La sera lenta come il viola
lenta come le siringhe, la sera lenta come la sera cade
disuguale come le spiree, come le siringhe, come la sera.

Riposerà nella notte il viola caduto, l'ombra caduta;
si sazierà d'ombra il piacere disuguale della sera.
Disuguale questo piacere nella sera riempito di aromi
sazierà la sera disuguale…
Dalla sera, dalle
siringhe, delle spiree ricurve
lenta la viola
salirà con onde
ricurve,
ricurva ombra
d'aromi.

VIOLET IS NOT A COLOR

Violet of the syringas and slow
        like the spireas of the curved waves
slow like violet the syringas
        fall unevenly.
Evening slow like violet
slow like the syringas, evening slow like evening falling
unevenly like the spireas, like the syringas, like the evening.

The fallen violet, the fallen shadow, will rest in the night;
evening's uneven pleasure will sate itself on shadow.
Uneven in the evening this pleasure filled with aromas
will sate the uneven evening…
From the evening, from
the syringas, slowly the violet
of the curved spireas
will rise in curved
waves,
curved shadow
of aromas.

GYPSOPHILA

a L. Anceschi

Dove sere di confini tormentosi
rovesciano fatiche immani, e si crogiola la follia dentro
il seme dell'aster, nell'altea insaziata, dove
geme una storia d'inibizioni, un
piano perde
il suo peso.
Vai dentro i corpicini della nebbia, corri mentre
è buio e sfuma i fioricini di nebbia.
Spilli d'aria bucano la corsa, il giardino si apre,
di là c'è una terra e ci latrano i cani.
Dietro ancora il suo buio fan gemme le rose,
e il vapore non soffia nel vuoto.
Nel luogo che la nebbia introduce
Primum aurora novo cum spargit lumine terras,
et variae volucres nemora avia pervolitantes
aera per tenerum liquidis loca vocibus opplent,
quam subito soleat sol ortus tempore tali
convestire sua perfundens omnia luce,
omnibus in promptu manifestumque esse videmus.
Una luce di uccelli solari riverbera l'aria
si stanzia nel luogo che non è.

GYPSOPHILA[1]

to L. Anceschi

Where evenings of tormenting boundaries
turn immense toil upside down, and folly revels inside
the seed of the aster, inside the insatiable althaea, where
a story of inhibitions moans, a
plan loses
its weight.
Go inside the tiny bodies of the mist, run while
it's dark and blur mist's tiny flowers.
Pins of air pierce the run, the garden opens,
there is a land on the other side and dogs bark there.
Behind its darkness buds burst on the roses again,
and vapor does not blow into the void.
In the place which mist ushers in
as soon as dawn suffuses earth with new splendor,
and motley birds flying through remote forests
in the soft sky fill the world with song,
how quickly the sun, just then risen,
covers all things sprinkling them with its light.
This sight and clear vision is known to all men.[2]
A light of solar birds reverberates air
settles in the place which does not exist.

A CAMPANA

Come bianco il come e il quando
        si tace
    bianco come quando
allora dai vichi marini il poeta se ne andava e la sera
andava con il poeta lassù come quando il poeta—
Bianco si tace e il
poeta e la sua sera se ne vengono meno al desiderio
bianco dell'uso e sul cammino disfatto dell'uso
ruota la scintilla bianca e nuova scende la sera
bianca su tutti gli occhi del mondo.

TO CAMPANA[1]

How white the why and the when
        keeps silent
    white as when
long ago the poet went away from the alleys by the sea
    [and evening
went with the poet high up as when the poet—
White keeps silent and the
poet and his evening forsake the white
desire of habit and on the worn-out road of habit
the spark rolls white and evening descends new
white upon all the eyes of the world.

CHI

Quando chi è se è
scoprirà tutte le voglie di questa pagina bianca
del sole di marzo dalle due e un quarto alle tre
o sniderà primule (gialle, solo foglie
un po' asciutte)—
quando lo farà
vedremo—
sarà in grado ancora—
        privi di forme—al caldo del sole—
        sentiamo passi di insetti
        smuoversi d'aria—
    di rintracciare pazienza in chiaroscuro
        linee di beneplaciti
        gli asserimenti del vuoto
            del desiderio?

WHO

When will he who is if he is
discover all the yearnings of this page white
with March sun from quarter past two to three
or rouse the primroses (yellow, only leaves
somewhat dry)—
we shall see
when he does—
or be capable again—
          devoid of form—in the heat of the sun—
          we hear insects' steps,
          shuffling of air—
     to retrace patience in chiaroscuro
          the lines of consent
          the declarations of the void
               of desire?

L'ANIMA DEL VEGETALE

Sembra che la voglia sia—per cambiare—
    un po' di sole
    mentre acceca la tua mente di topo
    persuasivo;
    nausea un tanto—un tanto
      quanto
o noia di sé—
    l'io cresce i viticchi—si sforza sempre
      poverino
    di trovare cosa lo faccia rantolare meglio.
Questi splendidi racemi e vilucchi dell'io—
    vegetalissimo—
        si-cu-ra-men-te
    vegetale,
    che perdura—in sogno a citare
i suoi scopi di vita—
Aglaia ed Eufrosine,
carissime—
    dove avete nascosto le vesti—
Sotto le siepi si attarda—
    io-tu
    vegetali—
e possiamo sperare di nuovo che anche

THE VEGETATIVE SOUL

It seems—for a change—that desire is
    for a bit of sun
  while it blinds your mind of suasive
    mouse;
  a bit of nausea—a tiny
    bit
or weariness of itself—
the "I" grows tendrils—strives always hard
    poor little thing
to find what makes it rattle better.
These splendid clusters and bindweeds of the "I"—
  the most vegetable "I"—
        cer-tain-ly
    vegetable,
  which keeps naming—in dream
    the scope of its life—
    Aglaia[1] and Euphrosyne,[2]
    my darlings—
        where have you hidden your clothes—
    Under the hedges lingers—
        the "I"-you
        vegetable—
    and let us hope once again that

le piante si colgano nell'essere che è
    che l'anima ce l'hanno
    che l'anima
        enti
        ce l'hanno.

the plants too surprise themselves in the being that is
>   for soul they have
>   for soul
>>   existence
>>   they have.

UNA SORTE

In una sorte da pochi spiccioli
in una carta di due
in una velina azzurra—
        ti si son trovate tutte le conferme:
        le partenze per ogni stazione,
        gli approdi per ogni riva,
        brusii—
                silenzio—
Così, fatto fagotto, la lirica si alza da tavola,
riparte sola; via tutti—
        la guida, il
        mattiniero vestito,
        il sanrocchino.
    Chiama senza sorriso / Sorride al
        una diana oscura / sommo de l'ascesa.

A FORTUNE

In a fortune worth two cents
in a deuce
in a blue onion-skin—
       you find all the confirmations:
       the departures for every station,
       the landings for every shore,
       buzzing—
            silence—
Thus, packed, the lyric leaves the table,
departs again alone; everyone out—
       the guide, the
       morning dress,
       the duffle coat.
     Without a smile / Smiles at
        a dark diana calls / the top of the ascent.

IN CONCLUSIONE

Coraggiosamente troviamo il punto
    ma traverso le impannate
dietro una tenda
        dietro di me —
            così semplicemente
troviamo il punto per uno, o due, o tre,
dispiaceri.

Come non segni
    una voluta di fumo
pensa da sé
attraversa anziani oggetti
    si adocchiano
la pretesa inutile del pensiero.

Che differenza (se)
    la coppettina
    il giochetto piccolo
        della nostra razza
    il farmi voce
permettono.

IN CONCLUSION

Bravely we find the point
    but through draped windows
behind a curtain
        behind me—
                so easily
we find the point for one, or two, or three
displeasures.

Just as you cannot pin
    a curl of smoke
the vain claim of the mind
thinks by itself
pierces ancient objects
    that eye one another.

What difference (if)
    a small glass
    the little game
        of our people
    gives me
voice.

Che una ansiosissima dialettica
se ne vada,
che la resoluzione più spinta
abdichi
che il giardino rinsecchi.

Let a most anxious dialectic
leave,
let the boldest resolution
abdicate
let the garden wither.

Resta il confine, e non sperare più, per
ancora sperare se dietro l'ombra del cardo
e nella siepe fitta, se dove l'ombra si cresce
di sé disposta—se davanti ombra ti veste
e scivoli rapido per lo stupore del nulla.
Le bambine si levano giocando e
di niente si vestono e nell'ombra che ti tiene
vanno senza peso e dentro l'ombra
che le tiene vanno in un gioco di bambole
dal campo alla siepe, nell'ombra
del cardo—la siepe che fitta si chiude
il nulla.

The boundary remains, and no more hope, no
hope anymore if behind the shadow of the thistle
and inside the thick hedge, if where the shadow grows
of its own accord—if in front the shadow covers you
and you slide swiftly out of amazement at the nothing.
The little girls get up and play and
cover themselves in nothing and inside the shadow that holds you
they go without weight and inside the shadow
that holds them they go as in a dolls' game
from field to hedge, in the shadow
of the thistle—the hedge that tightly closes
the nothing.

Di quale nitido stupore t'inchini, e a
distanza di sere ridistendi un animo
sempre più labefatto, non assediato
dall'edera, e percorso dai rumori e dagli
echi delle cose. Un assenzio verissimo—
ma incontrollata è la luce—ti bagna
le labbra e incespichi e cammini e dimori
e affondi nel cielo vertiginoso.
Lì ti sfrigola addosso ogni uccello
un usignolo con canti di memoria
ti grida se vai, ti accende e
stordisce nuovi ricordi.
L'assenza ti gira attorno, sei visto.
E sei un'ignita essenza.

You bow with such neat astonishment, and at
a distance of evenings you unfold again a spirit
more and more sunken, not besieged
by ivy, but trodden by the noises and
echoes of things. The truest absinthe[1]—
but the light is uncontrolled—moistens
your lips and you stumble and walk and linger
and sink into the vertiginous sky.
There every bird sputters,
a nightingale with songs of remembrance
shouts whether you go, kindles
new memories, deafening you.
Absence whirls around you, you are seen.
And you are a burning essence.

Trionfo di me, mi affondo
non libera e reduce da smisurate fortune
avvampo di pietà, galleggio nell'insofferenza.
In un caos di nubi incendiate si incendia la mia rivolta
mentre cerco di parlare qualcuno non c'è a sentire
e la menzogna della menzogna della menzogna
si appiatta dentro le volte celesti dell'ego.
Un incendio è l'immagine, ma il suo contrario
ugualmente avvampa in territori interiori che neanche l'io
percorre. Una catena l'immagine di due.
Un trionfo della solitudine, la delicieuse ivresse della
corrispondenza? Se qualcuno ascolta, che non sia pigro.
Rivoltato e incendiato nella rivolta, sgusci le metafore,
le riponga al sole.
Essenze caldissime, luci d'oro
non saranno offerte barocche, ma tagli
e sussurri, percorrimenti e whispers saranno profumo di
quel che ha cercato.

    His rebus dictis, è meglio incominciare:
Terre di lavande, nubi di flochs, venti
di daucon, abissi di maggi e serpentarie,
palazzi di betulle, non vi chiama Queen Mab. Ma
corrispondenze come memorie nel sonno e ombre

I triumph over myself, I triumph, I sink
not free but veteran from endless fortunes
I blaze with compassion, float in impatience.
My revolt takes fire in a chaos of burning clouds
I try to speak no one listens
and the lie of a lie of another lie
hides inside the celestial vaults of the ego.
Fire is an image, but its opposite
also blazes in inner territories which not even the "I"
can tread upon. A chain the image of two.
A triumph of the solitude, the *délicieuse ivresse* of
correspondence? If someone listens, let him not be lazy.
Revolted and set on fire by revolt, let him shuck the metaphors,
display them in the sun.
The warmest essences, lights of gold
will not be baroque offerings, but scraps
and murmurs, quiverings and *whispers* will be the perfume of
the one who has tried.
   Now, having said this,[1] it's better to begin:
Lands of lavenders, clouds of phlox, winds
of wild carrots, chasms of laburnum and serpentaria,
birch palaces, Queen Mab is not calling you. But
correspondences like memories inside sleep and shadows

nelle memorie del sonno, sonno intero della memoria
e corrispondenza di memoria e sonno;
gestazione d'oblio, memoria adunatrice di nomi, la
portiera di specchi e riflessioni.

in the memories of sleep, whole sleep of the memory
and correspondence of memory and sleep;
gestation of oblivion, memory summoner of names,
doorkeeper of mirrors and reflections.

SAGGIO FISICO DELL'INSTABILITÀ

Ondeggiare fluire
fluisce il dubbio fluisce la noia
coperte di dubbio ammantano un
paesaggio popolato fiorite dell'onda
respiri del dubbio fiorite del tema
dentro l'onda fiorita di
una passione annoiata.

PHYSICAL TEST OF INSTABILITY

Wavering flowing
doubt flows weariness flows
layers of doubt cover a
peopled landscape flowerings of the wave
sighs of doubt flowerings of the fear
inside the flowering wave of
a weary passion.

Luce nel vetro dolce di una luce
chiara chiama il vento pellegrino
di una persona stanca. Piaceri di mani,
curve di bocche tengono nel vento un luogo
dei sospiri. L'ultima figura danza il
desiderio, si spegne l'ultimo, si muta ratto nel voltarsi
limpido della luce.
Luce che soccombe in vetri dolci, che tende il vuoto
in un vuoto di luoghi, che deraglia in nubi grigie, che
si sfinisce in soffi di aliti celesti, che si combina in
percorsi d'aria, che si scioglie in rullii d'ombra,
che si sporge in creste di fiocchi bleu, che si drizza in
pastori erranti, che si incorpora in giganti, che si lancia
selvaggia, e si sfa dove passa il vento la luce oscura della
pioggia delle piogge che verranno.
Luce che spezza l'aria selvaggia che spazza nubi e voglie
e ripide figure. Oltre non tiene un rigor dolce di fiocchi
e di spinte la stanchezza.

Light of a clear light on the soft pane
summons a weary person's
peregrine wind. Delights of hands,
curves of mouths hold a place of sighs
in the wind. The last figure dances
desire, the last one to die, changes swiftly
in the limpid turning of the light.
Light that succumbs on the soft panes, that extends the void
in a void of places, that derails in grey clouds,
that wastes away in whiffs of celestial breaths, that mingles in
stretches of air, that melts in rollings of shadow,
that leans over crests of blue flakes, that rises in
wandering shepherds, that takes body in giants, that hurls itself
wild and gets undone where the wind goes by the dark light of the
rain of the rains-to-come.
Light that snaps the wild air sweeping away clouds and desires
and precipitous figures. Weariness holds nothing else
beyond a gentle harshness of flakes and thrusts.

Di una benevola oblivione, di una
malcerta fraternità, scandiamo prova su prova,
saggiando prove trepide di pensiero:
reggerà allo sforzo, al silenzio imperioso. alla
cara insensibilità?
Ripetendo il già detto e risentendo
del tutto il grigiore perenne, dove dentro i sassi di zolfo, come
si nasconde e prepara: nuovi viaggi; i
cicli nuovi, paesaggi mascherati in bouganvilles schiumose, in
    [verde
profuso alle balaustre bianche alle isole bianche ai sentieri
bianchi in pendio, al sole bianco che torna, al viaggio che
compare, e chi prepara i viaggi compare e scompare e non
torna, chi prepara di un Thume possente
scalpitii e sonnolenze, dolci amarognole fraternità, opaco
splendore, scompare dopo l'ultimo sonno, né
torna, a ridire, del cuore che c'è.
E quello ritorna e insorge d'opulenza e
lusso, ricolmo di fasti di fiori,
e tutti i serti del mondo circondano il suo pingue apparire.

Let us scan proof upon proof
of a benevolent oblivion, of a precarious brotherhood,
examining proofs trembling with thought:
will it withstand the effort, the haughty silence, the
cherished indifference?
Repeating what was already said and listening entirely
again to the perennial drabness where, inside the rocks of sulphur,
he hides and prepares: new voyages; new
cycles, landscapes masqueraded in foaming bougainvillaes, in green
profusion on white rails on white islands on white
steep paths, on the white sun which returns, on the voyage
that appears, and the one who prepares the voyages appears and
    [disappears and doesn't
return, the one who prepares the trampling and somnolence
of a powerful *Thume*,[1] bittersweet brotherhood, dull
splendor, disappears after the last sleep, nor does he come
back to tell again of the heart's existence.
And he returns rising in opulence and
luxury, loaded with gifts with flowers,
and all the wreaths in the world surround his rich appearing.

FIORI PER TE,
NEL TUO ANNIVERSARIO

Sereno, né sereno il luccicore
di un mazzetto che attende e non andrà,
candore e rose, e non andrà
negli androni sepolti in cui rischio
di credere che non ci sei
rischio di credere né voglio che ti si
anneghi il corpo che non
rifiorisca che non divampi
come l'aneto... quando le lucciole dei
boschi e i lati fioriti nella valle si
alzeranno in disteso splendore (rischio
di credere che non si anneghi) splendo di sole e
il sole mi presta il volere—anche se è notte
dentro il sole che avvampa
nelle tue rose, nelle lucciole bianche,
nei petali bianchi, nei lumi di fresie,
nei lumi del bianco, sei per dire qui,
che ancora
così andiamo tu ed io.
È riprendendo della vita il suo lato
fiorito, non potrai dire facciamo,
non potrai dire andiamo—
sola parlo con il tuo silenzio.

FLOWERS FOR YOU,
ON YOUR ANNIVERSARY

Bright, not bright the glitter
of a bouquet that waits but won't go,
whiteness and roses, and it won't go
into the buried passages in which I risk
to believe you are not
risk to believe nor do I want
to believe that your body may drown may not
bloom again may not blaze forth
like dill… when the fireflies
of the forests and the flowering hillsides
rise in uninterrupted splendor (I risk
to believe it won't drown) I shine with sun and
the sun lends me the will—even if it's night
inside the splendent sun
inside your roses, inside the white fireflies,
inside the white petals, inside the lights of freesias,
inside the lights of the white, you are, as it were, here
for we still
go like this you and I.
And to resume the flowery side
of life, you won't be able to say let's do,
you won't be able to say let's go—
alone I speak with your silence.

Il tempo è dolce, ma non fremere é sfioccarsi di tutti i sì
nebbiarsi di corolle e non giungere più
nonostante che tu ducis in longum amores—

Dolce il tempo, chiara quest'ora—
silet aequor, silet nox
silet—

E chiara come luna flebile e serena che
sfiocca nei sì quanto di sé langue
senza rumore—
dolce,

Et nunc omne tibi stratum silet aequor, et omnes,
adspice… senza fruscii il cuore piega verso di te—
ventosi ceciderunt murmuris aurae.

The weather is fair, but not to quiver is an unravelling of all yesses
a clouding of corollas and not to reach anymore
even though—*you drag out our love*[1]

Fair weather, clear hour—
the sea lies silent—[2] *the night lies silent*[3]
silent[4]

And clear like a weak, calm moon
unraveling into yesses all that languishes inside her
without noise—
softly,

And now stretched before you, the sea lies silent,
and look...[5] *without rustlings the heart bends towards you—*
all the breaths of the murmuring wind have ceased.[6]

Guarda, tutto ritorna, anche i segni nel muro
e dietro le siepi gli occhi dei nostri paradisi
senza ragione d'esserci volgono a tornare,
ritornano per non dimenticare, quanto trae
ciascuno il suo piacere—e adspice:
anche se a me tuttavia: perché la sera volge,
e l'anno fermenta nelle case, e si dispongono tutti
ad uscire i ragazzi sulle strade, e scendono tutti
per il loro amore: chi si guarda e chi, fuori
del buio, nella luce si prende e gli occhi
puntati nel cuore della luce: il silenzio
brillante della luce, l'ascolto.
Chi non si è accorto che non c'è tregua,
e che incessante brucia, ciascuno a suo piacere.
Così, dopo che ha visto, ciascuno la sua luce,
brucia la propria insania nell'ombra, e riesce,
nel lucore, come vite frondosa.
Mentre parliamo il silenzio volge nella sera
et sol crescentis decedens duplicat umbras:
e tuttavia brucia, e richiama
una stagione non nata, la stagione che non
volge né ritorna, il passo senza misura,
di anno senz'anni, e semprevivi,

Look, everything returns, even the signs on the wall,
and, behind the hedges, the eyes of our paradises
with no reason to be there are wont to turn back,
they turn back not to forget the pleasure which
everyone derives—and *look!*:[1]
even if to me however: because night turns,
and the year ferments in the homes, and all the youngsters get
ready to go out into the streets, and they all come down
for their love: the ones who gaze at each other and the ones, outside
the darkness, who grab in the light, their eyes pinned
to the heart of the light: the bright
silence of the light, the listening.
The ones who don't realize that there's is no truce,
and that everyone burns incessantly at his pleasure.
Thus, after each has seen his light,
he burns his own folly in the shade, and steps out again,
in the dim light, like a leafy vine.
While we speak, silence turns in the night
and the setting sun doubles the growing shadows:[2]
and yet it still burns and calls back
an unborn season, the season that neither
turns nor returns, the measureless step
of the yearless year; and sempervivums,[3]

piante perenni, che come succhia il tempo
le sue linfe gonfie si gettino al rigoglio
dell'amore che brucia.

perennial plants that, when time draws forth
their swollen sap, fling themselves into the exuberance
of the burning love.

Quae nemora aut qui vos saltus habuere puellae
Naides, indigno cum Gallus amore peribat?

Chi si strugge anche ora, tanto che poi lo piangono
i lauri (etiam flevere myricae, pinifer illum etiam
sola sub rupe jacentem), che poi anche le tamerici,
che giace sotto la rupe, lo piangono.
Chi e dove, se non nella terra del nulla, nel dove non
nel non ruscelli nel non alberi nel non citisi e
lacrime nel non bacche rubenti del minio e dell'ebbio—
nella terra d'un non inscritto in tutti i pertugi che si
serve d'oblio e memoria, che si va nel vuoto perenne dove sconf
e fronde accompagnano, tu desiderante e io, non é il
dialogo giusto, ma tentante ancora si produce.
Dove tu con le regioni coperte di neve, con i fuochi
d'autunno e la capre sui pendii e le molte passeggiate
in vie e su tetti impossibili e chiari, dove le regioni
si svuotano, diventano miniere, si ascoltano i juke box,
si guardano ansanti ragazzi in gioco, si esaltano, si
prendono e si precipitano le siepi dietro le siepi
allacciate in nessuna collina, in colline di seni duri,
che palpitano in soli meridiani, e dove le meridiane
faci non son viste e si vedono, solo da chi sa

*What groves, what glades held you, water
nymphs, when Gallus was pining with a love unrequited?*[1]

Who pines even now, pines so much that later the laurels
weep for him (*even the tamarisks, even the pines, wept for him,
as he lay below a lonely cliff*)[2], and afterwards also the tamarisks
weep for him lying below the cliff.
Who and where, if not in the land of nothing, in the nowhere
in the nonstreams in the nontrees in the nonbrooms and
tears in the purple nonberries of the elder and cinnabar
in the land of one not engraved in every crevice, who makes
use of oblivion and memory, who goes into the perennial void where
sorrow and fronds attend, you desiring and I, it is not the
right dialogue, but groping it still occurs.
Where you with the regions covered with snow, with autumn
fires and goats on the slopes and the many walks
on streets and on impossible, clear rooftops, where the regions
become empty, become mines, juke boxes are heard,
panting youngsters gaze at each other playfully, extol and
grab each other and hedges rush into hedges
tied to no hill, on hills of hard breasts
that throb under noon suns, and where the bright
lights are not seen and yet can be seen only by one who knows

85

le strade del fuoco, dove i gatti si occhieggiano,
s'arruffano dove un'impertinenza si prodiga
nella disperazione e il calcolo si sviluppa,
si dà, si muta, si finisce, e si scopre ingenuità da due soldi.
La terra dove si strugge anche ora, tanto che poi lo piangono
dolci coi lauri le tamerici, e le nebbie accorate dallo
spavento si germogliano: più teneri vilucchi di vitalbe
e l'aneto ricompare, bombardando il calcolo di
mille ossessioni, uccidendo il calcolo producendo
reti di ragno infinite, e memorie di un io inoggettivo
che non sentenzia, e si cerca la casa
sul pendio, la casa sotto la rupe,
il fossato dove a giorno piano o a notte crescente
animate escono le lepri a danzare, e si danza anche
l'io oscuro, senza lacci con ornamenti silvestri
sul capo, con l'ebbio e il minio purpurei, nel sangue
delle bacche intriso il capo desiderante e prezioso,
che si strugge, per non morire più, per non
vedere il fulcro degli amori che scompare, che si scioglie
senza più lasciare traccia.
(Unde amor iste—tibi—quid, insanis, tua cura...)
Di dove l'amore ti viene, perché, l'insania d'una terra
del nulla, ubriaco di nulla riesci a colpire occhi e mani,
e collo, e torce la mente solida che assuefatta al
calcolo dormiva di numeri sennati la pace di notti lunghe e ora
riempie di volti che chiamano e occhi, e mani nuove, le notti
o il meridiano torpore, o dilaga senza più sonno, nei

the roads of fire, where cats eye one another,
scuffle, where sauciness is bestowed
in despair, and calculation grows,
gives, changes, ends, and discovers in itself a naïveté worth two bits.
The land where he pines even now, pines so much that later
    [the tamarisks
weep for him softly with the laurels, and heartbroken by
fear mists sprout: the tenderest clematis vines
and the dill reappear, bombarding calculation with
a thousand obsessions, killing calculation, spinning
infinite spider webs, and memories of a nonobjective "I"
that does not judge, and looks for the home
on the slope, the home below the cliff,
the ditch where in drawn-out day or in growing night
lively the rabbits come out to dance, and the dark "I" also
dances, without ties with wild ornaments
on its head, with the purple elder and the cinnabar, the
desiring and precious head drenched in the blood of berries,
pines not to die anymore, not to
see loves' fulcrum disappear, dissolve
leaving no trace.
(*Whence this love of thine? What madness this? Your beloved...*)³
Where does your love come from, why the folly for a land
of nothing, drunk with nothing you manage to strike eyes and hands
and neck. Folly twists the solid mind that, inured to
calculation, was sleeping in wise rhythms the peace of long nights
    [and now
fills the nights or noon numbness with wailing faces and eyes and
    [new
hands, or spreads, not sleepy anymore, into the

midolli teneri dell'io privo di responsabilità?
Extremum hunc, Arethusa, mihi concede laborem
come di chi è fuori di sé dirà l'amore, nelle midolla
tenere lo spino ficcato consapevole o no,
tra stasi e desiderio, lo scuotimento ansima,
domina il soggetto. E tu, Arethusa,
di tutto un po', parlando le vie dorate del nulla concludi,
e dominando l'occlusione dei sensi
termina per il piacere ciò che non è stato
per il dovere concluso.

soft marrow of the "I" devoid of responsiblity?
Grant to me this most difficult task, Arethusa,[4]
like to one who, beside himself, aware or not of the thorn
embedded in the soft marrow, panting in anxiety between
 [languour and desire,
recounts how love overcomes the subject. And you,
Arethusa, speaking of this or that, come to the end of the
golden roads of the nothing
and, overcoming the occlusion of the senses,
fulfill for pleasure what was not
fulfilled for duty.

Come le nature morte
nel tempo perduto, nell'infanzia che si
sveste, nel tempo riempito, nel tempo
finito, nel tempo che si compie, nel tempo che
si lascia, nel tempo che si crea, nel tempo che
si fa, che si vende, che si nasce, che si vuota, che si
        trastulla
negl'innumeri tempi che non abbiamo
    che non ci è dato incollare a pagine bianche,
        che non possiamo ammettere, che non dovremo sentire,
    che non sentiamo aprire, che vorremmo
        gaudere
né possiamo avviare il tempo, inquadrare lo
spazio, spingere il tempo, far suonare lo spazio,
ritardare il tempo, circumscrivere spazio,
darci il nostro
        tempo
né uccidendo, sentendo, sfacendo, serbando,
scordando, arrischiando, chiamando, chiedendo,
        pensando
avviamo quel tempo, mangiamo quel tempo,
azzardiamo in un tempo di vincite, perdite
        roulettes e tamburi,
    il tempo
    finito che si sia.

Like still lifes
in lost time, in the childhood that
strips itself, in filled time, in finite
time, in the time that ticks by, in the time left
behind, in the time that begets, in the time that
becomes, that expends, that is born, that gets empty, that
      lingers on
in the innumerable times we do not have
    which we are not given to paste on white pages,
    which we cannot acknowledge, which we shall not hear,
    which we don't hear open, which we wish
      to enjoy
neither can we set time going, nor frame
space or push time, make space resound,
slow down time, *circumscribe*[1] space,
give ourselves
    time
neither by killing, feeling, undoing, keeping,
neither by forgetting, risking, calling, asking,
    thinking
can we set that time going, eat that time,
risk in a time of profits, losses
      roulettes and drums,
    time
    finite as it may be.

Denique, nos ipsi caecis quaecumque tenebris,
tangimus
  Di quale colore qui
         distesi di quale
 quod quoniam vinco
si tango.
   Come di quale, di quale, di quale
   colore
    distenderai
    nelle tenebre degli occhi
    toccando
    forma senza colore
    ma caecis quaecumque tenebris
 non insegneremo le forme e i colori
o le curve immobili
    d'un'ipomea azzurra
    nelle tenebre bianche
    delle foglie bianche
    d'un bel libro.
Eppure:
 fieri nunc esse docebo.
E come finalmente
  cuori e fantasie così molli
  che come nelle tenebre
    quaecumque—nescis?

Again, whatever ourselves may touch in sightless darkness...[1]
    What color   here
                                stretched what
   since I conquer,
   if I touch[2]
     Like what color, what, what
     color
        will you stretch forth
        in the darkness of the eyes
        touching
        form without color
        but *whatever in sightless darkness*[3]
we shall not teach the forms and the colors
or the motionless curves
        of a blue morning glory
        in the white darkness
        of the white leaves
        of a beautiful book.
And yet:
   now I'll show how it is.[4]
And how finally
   hearts and fantasies so soft
   that are as if in darkness
      whatever—don't you know?[5]

In fratte e rive d'orti,
in messe o battitura o vendemmia o potagione
o tagliatura di legne, o pastura di greggi
o d'armenti, o cura d'api o di fratte o di
fossi o di rivi o d'orti o uccellagione.
Invenias
    piaceri assenti, tenebre molli,
    dove caecigeni, solis qui lumina numquam
        (poveri da sempre)
    dispexere,
    faranno le esequie
    dei corpi, e si ricorderanno
    di tutto, di ciò che si sente,
    nei colori congiunti, di tante
    favole d'uomo.
Come sempre rursum allora
    docebo così come è,
    sui molli cuori delle tenebre
    dei libri, che
    le corde più vive di
    uomini ciechi
    si aprono in cuori molli
    e presenti il pensiero di
    questo libro
        infinito.

  Lucrezio, *De retum natura*, vv. 745–46, libro II.
  Interpolazioni in diversi punti di questo passo del libro II in cui L. dimostra che anche al buio, per l'aggregazione degli atomi, accade che pur non distinguendo i colori, possiamo individuare i corpi.
  A parte come il presentimento d'una discussione posteriore di secoli, del sensismo, sulle possibilità dell'uomo, privato d'alcuni suoi sensi, o a

In bushes and at gardens' edges,
in crops or threshing or vintage or tree pruning
or cutting of wood, or in pastures of sheep
or herds, or keeping of bees, or bushes or
ditches or streams or gardens or bird shooting.
May you find[6]
>absent pleasures, soft darkness,
>*where those who are blind from birth,*
>>(the forever poor)
>
>*who have never looked on the sunlight...*[7]
>will perform the funeral rites for
>the bodies and remember
>everything one senses
>in the mingled colors of so many
>tales of man.

Then as usual, *I will show again* [8]
>just how it is,
>about the soft hearts of the books'
>darkness, how
>the most lively chords
>of blind men
>open in soft and present
>hearts the thought of
>this infinite
>>book.

Lucretius, *De rerum natura*, II, 745–46.

Interpolations at different points in this passage of Book II in which Lucretius proves that, because of the aggregation of atoms, it happens, that even in darkness, when we cannot distinguish colors, we can locate the bodies.

Leaving sensism aside as a foreboding of an argument that would come

nudo, « naturale », per così dire, concepito in uno stato di privazione di conoscenza d'alcun genere, ed esaminato nelle sue reazioni di fronte agli oggetti colpisce, in Lucrezio, l'immagine angosciosa, poeticissima, della « cecità » delle tenebre, che è cecità dell'uomo.

Sotto simboli, se ne trae un'immagine della vulnerabilità assoluta, dell'essere umano, che trionfa e s'inorgoglisce quanto pure crede di poter trionfare di qualche sua conquista: « quod quoniam vinco, (si tango) fieri nunc esse docebo »...

Forma senza colore: 'The hollow men': Shape Without form, shade without colour ecc., ma con un'eco dantesca, di qualche visione teologica.

L'ipomea azzurra è un bel fiore, nelle pagine del libro non è un'abitudine romantica, ma il segno di una conservazione nel tempo, impossibile.

Il libro è poi un termine di riferimento importante: è dove si ritrovano spazi e tempi degli uomini: ciò che è stato da loro voluto, desiderato, fermato con una scrittura.

Dunque ciò che si sente « vivo »: le foglie bianche (si gioca perciò sulle parole); ma anche ciò che si sa « prodotto », e quasi anche figlio del tempo, nonostante tutto, morto.

Anche se si trionfa della morte, tuttavia resta l'illusione del « fieri nunc esse docebo ».

E l'illusione contrasta ancora drammaticamente con la mollezza del nostro cuore, con una fantasia pronta a tutto, che la partorisce, e viene falcidiata dalla crudeltà della sua fine: che è fine della vita, come della fantasia, come dell'orgoglio: di tutto.

Cuori e fantasie molli: la dicitura è leopardiana, tratta da un passo del « Discorso di un italiano intorno alla poesia romantica ».

Continua però ancora per un po' il gioco dell'illusione fantastica: direttamente da un poeta amato, che parla dei *motivi* della poesia: indicazioni di desiderio che stupisce di nature integre e felici, che sa gettare le parole più vaghe sugli oggetti dell'uso quotidiano onde farne cose della poesia, con quel tanto di incantagione che deriva da un uso di termini leggermente antiquati, già saturi di classicità di lingua, già pregni di storia umana e letteraria: da L. brano già citato.

Quel che si potrà trovare, dopo questo inganno, e questo lasciarsi andare del cuore, sarà forse il vuoto: come piacere assente, come tenebra, che ci scopre ancora i « poveri da sempre », i caecigeni per nascita, che dopo aver fatto le esequie dei loro corpi manterranno di sé, solo povere (o preziose?) memorie: le memorie delle favole d'uomo.

Così può continuare allora la storia, ripetendo di nuovo il processo: dall'insegnare però, questa volta, la realtà dei cuori molli, degli uomini ciechi, attraverso il pensiero di ciò che nella vita si trae come in un libro infinito.

Per i poveri: tutte le metafore bibliche ed evangeliche del « povero ».

Per il libro infinito: ciò che per l'universo si squaderna: Dante, Paradiso, canto XXXIII, v. 87.

up later in the centuries (the possibility that man, deprived of some of his senses, or naked, or "natural" so to speak, conceived in a state devoid of any kind of knowledge and tested for his reactions before the objects), what strikes the reader in Lucretius is the most poetical, anxiety-laden image of the "blindness" of darkness, which is also the blindness of man.

Beneath the symbols, one gets an image of the absolute vulnerability of the human being who triumphs and takes pride at the same time in his belief that he can triumph over some of his conquests: *Since I conquer, if I touch, I will demonstrate how it is.*[1]

Form without color: "The hollow men": "shape without form, shade without colour, etc.," but with a Dantesque echo of some theological vision.

The blue morning glory is a beautiful flower; in the pages of a book it is not a romantic habit, but the sign of an impossible preservation in time. Furthermore, the book is a term of important reference: it's where one finds the spaces and the times of men: what they wanted, desired, captured by means of writing. By extension, what one feels "alive": the white leaves (word play); but also that which is a "product" and also an offspring of time which, nevertheless, is dead.

Even if one triumphs over death, yet the illusion remains of *how it is.*[2]

And the illusion contrasts again dramatically with the softness of our hearts, with a fantasy ready for everything it gives birth to and is cut down by the cruelty of its end: which is the end of life, as well as of fantasy and pride: of everything.

Soft hearts and fantasies: the wording is taken from a passage by Leopardi on the "Discourse of an Italian on Romantic Poetry."

However, the game of fanciful illusion goes on for a while: it stems directly from a beloved poet who speaks of the motifs of poetry as the indications of a desire that is astonished at upright, happy natures, that knows how to fling the most graceful words on objects of daily use so as to turn them into poetry, with enough incantation which comes from the usage of slightly old-fashioned words, or of words saturated with classic idiom, already pregnant with human and literary histories: from Leopardi, as mentioned above.

What one can find after this deceit, and after this letting go of the heart, is perhaps the void: as absent pleasure, as darkness, which exposes us to ourselves as "the forever poor," the blind at birth, who—after having performed funeral rites for their bodies—will retain only pitiful (or precious) memories of themselves: the memories of man's tales.

Thus history can go on repeating again the process: however, this time it can do so by teaching the truth about the soft heart of man and by means of thoughts drawn from life as if it were an infinite book. For the poor: all the biblical and evangelical metaphors about the "poor."

For the infinite book: *ciò che per l'universo si squaderna*: Dante, *Paradiso*, canto XXXIII, l. 87.[3]

Vides, quanto all'immaginativa e al
desiderio nostro—
    indole, ingegno, offuscazione di cose naturali,
    snaturatezza d'una consuetudine,
    adsuefactus sum—non nego—
    basti la favella,
    possano le parole,
    con la forza pure di chi sa
scattare d'ira e d'ingegno, e di pensiero.

Come vedi, l'antichità nostra

    i secoli dei precedenti ingegni nostri
non ci bastano.
Ed omettendo pure di buona voglia
presagi dolorosi—
    parole non bastano
        per la ragione che
           non ho mentovato
    ma che è la ragione
        la ragione
    del desiderio nostro.

You see[1] concerning the power of imagination and
this desire of ours—
> nature, intelligence, a dimming of natural things,
> the inhumanity of a habit,
> *I have grown accustomed*—[2] I don't deny—
> speech may be enough,
> words may be able to,
> even with the force of one who knows how
to burst with rage and intelligence, and with thought.

As you see, our ancientness

> the centuries of our preceding intelligences
are not enough for us.
And even if we omit willingly
painful omens—
> words are not enough
>> for the reason
>> I have not mentioned
> but which is the reason
>> the reason
> for our desire.

Giallo la curva molle del vetro giallo
contro la coppa del vino il cigno di vetro.
Sul tavolo biondo rinfuse le carte
il cigno di vetro.

Ma di là nel sole asteres e cerasti più molli
    e clematidi in siepi di manine azzurre—
ma di là più molli daphni sericee, weigelie potenti—
    scuotono profumi.

E fumi odorosi d'erba sorgono alle mani—
quando le malve o l'appio verde
o il crespo aneto negli orti perio,
si ravviva un altr'anno e rifiorisce.

E ibridi corpi di flochs ci premono a fermarci.
(quale giardino fiorirà a primavera?
will it bloom this year?).

Dove le daphni di seta vedranno nell'ombra i tuoi passi vicini
premere l'erba—esalare ancora i fumi odorosi
    la pioggia recente.

Yellow, the soft curve of the yellow glass
against the wine cup the glass swan.
On the blond table helter-skelter the cards
the glass swan.

But over there in the sun asters and the softest chickweeds
    and clematis in hedges of tiny blue hands—
but over there the softest silk daphnes, powerful honeysuckle,
    scatter perfumes.

And scents of sweet-smelling grasses rise to our hands—
—when mallows or green lovage
or curly dill dead in the gardens,
one more year revives and blooms again.

And the hybrid bodies of phlox urge us to stop.
(what garden will bloom in the spring?
will it bloom this year?).

Where the silk daphnes will see in the shade your mincing steps
press down the grass—*the fragrant fumes* exhale again
    the last rain.

E piene le mani—manibus oh
  clematidi in siepi di mani piccine
  teneri cuori di lapis lazul a membrane.

Ma là dove lungo infinito ineccitabil sonno
ci porta, rifiorirà l'aneto?

Il dentro e il fuori, l'interno e l'esterno contrapposti sono i luoghi simbolici in cui possiamo vivere la vita, luoghi contrarii, naturalmente, per le presenze diverse che li animano.

Nel fuori: i fiori, talvolta, come accade per le clematidi, sono visti in un connubio umano o anche minerale (manine azzurre, lapislazzuli).

Tutti i sensi della storia del giardino vengono richiamati da questo giardino: valle dell'Eden, valle del Cantico dei Cantici, orto delle delizie, esercizio umano d'un'arte naturale; il giardino è recinzione di natura più preziosa, come composizione di piaceri per i sensi e lo spirito.

Così, colori, profumi, così perennità, caducità, assieme.

Nella terza strofa tre versi di Mosco, da Leopardi tradotti e inseriti nel Discorso di un Italiano intorno alla poesia romantica, in difesa della poesia classica. Alludono al rifiorire delle piante alla primavera e al dubbio rifiorire dell'uomo dopo la morte. Sono per Bione morto.

Ancora il giardino; i fiori ci invitano a fermarci qui, nella nostra vita: si insinua l'interrogativo delle religioni primitive, quelle dei cicli dell'eterno ritorno, secondo la ripresa, e nel senso che ne dà l'Eliot della « Terra desolata ».

Le daphni sono la presenza di una vita « altra » che a nostra insaputa ci spia, e forse ci « sente » in modo diverso dal nostro.

La persona è quella che ci vive abitualmente accanto, è « altra » persona, i cui segni sono fruscii, voci, passi, che lascia tracce (premere l'erba), e che ci è compagna nella morte.

Una voce allora di compianto per questa morte intravista si leva dal ricordo di Virgilio, Eneide, VI, vv. 883-4; e Dante, Purgatorio, XXX, vv. 19 e segg.; « Manibus o date lilia plenis », e da un coro di clematidi che nella siepe levano manine membranose (guarda le membrane dei petali delle clematidi). Guardane la forma, che in ischema ricorda un cuore.

Non resta dunque che tornare alla domanda che fiorisce da un Leopardi che si incrocia con l'alessandrino Mosco: se anche noi, nel « lungo ineccitabil sonno », rifioriremo come l'aneto.

And the hands full—*with hands*[1]
   clematis in hedges of tiny little hands
   tender hearts of webbed lapis lazuli.

But there where the long infinite impassive sleep
takes us, will dill bloom again?

    Set in opposition, the inside and the outside, the inner and the outer, are the symbolic loci in which we can live life; opposite places, of course, because of the different presences that give them life. About the outside: sometimes, as it happens with clematis, flowers are seen in a human or mineral partnership (tiny blue-hands, lapis lazuli).
    All the meanings of the garden story are recalled by this garden: the valley of Eden, the valley of the Song of Songs, the garden of delights, the human practice of nature art; the garden is the enclosure of a most valuable nature, a composition of pleasures for the senses and the spirit. And by the same token: colors, perfumes, and also everlastingness and transience.
    In the third stanza, three lines by Moschus, translated by Leopardi and included in his *Discourse of an Italian Concerning Romantic Poetry, in defense of classical poetry,* refer to the flowering of plants again in the spring and to man's dubious flowering again after death. The lines are dedicated to Bion on his death.
    Again the garden: flowers invite us to stop here, in the midst of our life. The garden suggests the questions asked by early religions, those with the cycles of the eternal return, in keeping with the remark and the meaning that T. S. Eliot gives it in *The Waste Land.*
    The daphnes are the presence of "another" life that, without our knowledge, is spying on us and perhaps "hears" us in a different way from our own.
    The person is the one who usually lives beside us, it is the "other"— whose signs are the rustlings, the voices, the steps—the one that leaves traces behind (by pressing the grass), our companion in death.
    A voice of regret, then, for this glimpsed death rises from Virgil's memory, *Aeneid,* vi, l. 883–4; and Dante, *Purgatory,* xxx, l. 19 and the following ones; "*Manibus date lilia plenis,*"[1] and from a choir of clematis that raise webbed little hands from the hedge (look at the webbed petals of clematis). Look at their shape which, in design, reminds one of a heart.
    Therefore, what's left is to return to the question that springs from Leopardi and which intersects the Alexandrian poet Moschus: whether we too, in the "*long, impassive sleep,*" will bloom again like dill.

SUAVIS TEMPESTAS

Stagione che formi i desideri che li porti
davanti alle case che ci conduci
dentro alle porte di Smirne o di Norchia che
tenti d'imporci nei sensi le tue vecchie questioni (che)
nei sensi
Timbri dei sensi e immagini di cose, semplici idee che tutto ci
spaura, semplici idee che
in estasi sintetiche il conoscere rapisce e che
talora s'ingannan per sentire le
voci dei bambini che cantano nella cupola e che
invece si ascoltano in lunghe melodie:
melanconiose e con allusioni tristi, lente lunghe
travestite, disperse ancora di
inquietudini che
nel tempo non si rassegnano a finire.

Stagione rapinosa che privi che tremi, che ci lasci come
secche appendici della terra, che distruggi e sopisci che
generi e ridai—dentro ai flutti del mare dentro le
chiazze di luce dove tremano le
foglie dove il pino si distende e assente alla brezza:
    —che ci apri che ci chiudi i nostri occhi—

SUAVIS TEMPESTAS[1]

Season, you shape desires you bring them
before the houses you lead us
inside the doors of Smyrna or of Norchia[2] you
try to impose your old questions on our senses (which)
on our senses
Timbre of the senses and images of things, simple ideas because
    [everything
frightens us, simple ideas which
knowledge ravishes in synthetic ecstasies and which
sometimes deceive out of desire to hear
the voices of children singing in the dome and who
hear one another instead in long melodies:
gloomy melodies and sad with allusions, slow long
disguised, suffused again
with anxieties which
do not resign themselves to cease in time.

Rapturous season, you strip, you shiver, you leave us
like dry appendages of the earth, you destroy and soothe,
you bring forth and give back—inside the swell of the sea inside the
splotches of light where the leaves
shiver where the pine tree stretches and nods in the breeze:
    —you open and close our eyes—

Stagione rapace che ha i cieli infaticabili dove
nuvole e chiari si accendono dove la fame di
azzurro e di rosso e di rosa e
di grigio si sazia di limiti più ricchi:
 —mobili infiniti argentei confini—

Stagione infinita come se d'infinito si discorre
 (si va nel desiderio): infinito piacere d'a-
scolto che
la giornata infinita di questa stagione ci porge
infinita statio degli anni, infinita
gioia ed angustia (infinita)
cagione di mutamenti e d'identificazioni.

(E tu, stagione « giuliva »?) (E tu, stagione
« fiorita »?) Verde
che gli anni contano e spuntano via via
col dito, che
non ci lasci più campare stagione infinita soave,
stagione che muti, che rompi le acque, le falde,
i fiumi, i rovinosi corsi dei fiumi, che
  incalzi:
scintille di luce in gocciole d'acqua, che
stupisci le bocche in carminei fremiti: che
incalzi i nostri piccoli animali: che
ci scuoti come ciondoli.
 —Che suavis natura —
 (le madri di tutte le cose…)
 —stagione delle meraviglie—

Rapacious season with untiring skies where
clouds and light catch fire, where the hunger
for blue and red and pink and
grey is fulfilled on more magnificent frontiers:
    —movable infinite silvery boundaries—

Infinite season, as if we discoursed about the infinite
    (we slip into desire): infinite delight of
listening which
this season's infinite day offers us
infinite *resting place*[3] of the years, infinite
joy and (infinite) anxiety
cause of changes and identifications.

(And you, "joyful" season?) (And you, "flowering"
season?)   Green
because the years count and tick gradually off
with a finger, because you
don't let us live anymore, gentle infinite season,
changing season, because you break the waters, the shallows,
the rivers, the ruinous watercourses, because you
    pursue:
sparks of light in water droplets, because you
astonish mouths in crimson quiverings: because you
pursue our tiny animals : because you
shake us like dangling trinkets.
    —Such *sweet nature*[4]—
    (mothers of all things…)
    —season of wonders—

Per cui
sufficiunt nobis et splendida lumina solis:
e molti, poi, stagione, per cui
son conti gli anni, (stagione beata che muti le penne), e di cui
nulla speme m'avanza: sicché:
il contemplatore,
l'uomo dei desideri, parte per naufragi
per opaca domorum, per i porti e le entrate di
quanto ci resta:
(e mentre
descrivi passando le immagini rotte
—son quel che s'è detto le broken images
del tempo—corri via,
    scivolati
        giù,
senza più contatori, senza più
contare il tuo tempo).

E molti sufficiunt, uomo dei desideri,
e mio uomo del tempo: molti sufficiunt
per darci consolazione: molti brandelli
d'immagini: coglili dentro gli opaca
domorum, le caverne opache
di Norchia:
specchi a pezzetti, libri e ceramiche,
stantuffi e cordame, (tutti nella caverna opaca,
nei porti dove muove il suo tempo
l'immagine rotta di ciò che ci avanza).

So that
even the blazing lights of the sun are enough for us:[5]
and many, then, season, so that
the years are numbered, (blessed season of changing feathers),
                                      and of which
no hope remains to me: so that:
the contemplative one,
the man of desires, departs for shipwrecks
for the shady dwelling places,[6] for the ports and the entryways of
what is left to us:
(and while
you describe by means of broken images
—what have been called the broken images
of time—you speed on,
    slipped
        away,
without meters, without
counting your time).

And many *are enough*,[7] man of desires,
and my man of time: many *are enough*,
to give us consolation: many scraps of
images: grab them inside the *shady dwelling
places*, inside Norchia's opaque
caves:
mirrors in smithereens, books and pottery,
rods and ropes, (everything inside the opaque cave,
inside the ports where your time moves
the broken image of what's left to us).

Spira il tuo tempo, alita il tempo:
brezza d'umori che il tufo innesca posando i desideri.
Splendida lumina solis, nella caverna,
splendida lumina ondeggiano; guizzano alle pareti:
hanno stimoli carnei.
Splendida lumina solis, qua dentro, dove
s'incrociano le tau
della Norchia perennis: stazione
dei desideri, tempestas degli anni,
stazione di porte e di porte, statio perennis
del tempo.

Stesi nel sole alberi della vita con tau,
tesi nel tufo nel tempo perenne,
incendiario delle luci del sole
praesertim cum tempestas adridet et anni
tempora conspergunt viridantis floribus herbas.

Queti nel sole
che sconvolgono i desideri di coloro
che dormono nei cuori del tufo.

Inganno felice d'una stagione perenne d'inganni.
Nostra Norchia quotidiana alla quale undique pervenimus
per il buio, alla porta, umili e proni a raccogliere
dietro, nel buio, tutte le immagini rotte, un po'
di segni, un po' duri a morire.

Undique, dunque, eccoci tutti qui,
facciamoci un po' di compagnia in queste anticamere

Breathe your time, breathe time:
breeze of humors which the tuff[8] baits while desires cease.
Inside the cave, *the blazing lights of the sun,*[9]
the blazing lights waver, dart on the walls:
have flesh-like stimuli.
The blazing lights of the sun, inside here, where
the tau's of *perennial*[10] Norchia
intersect: resting place
of desires, *season*[11] of the years,
resting place of doors and doors, *perennial resting place*[12]
of time.

Stretched in the sun tau-shaped trees of life,
stretched in the tuff in everlasting time,
incendiary of the sun's lights
especially when the season smiles and the time of year
sprinkles the fresh green grass with flowers.[13]

Quiet in the sun
they perturb the desires of those
who sleep in the heart of the tuff.

Happy deceit of a perennial season of deceits.
Our daily Norchia to whose door *we have arrived from everywhere*[14]
through darkness, humble and bent, to gather
behind, in the darkness, all the broken images, and a few
signs, somewhat slow to die.

From everywhere,[15] therefore, here we all are,
let us keep each other company in these antechambers

di Norchia care porte di tau,
cari cuori di abissi del tufo virente,
cari abissi senza stagioni, senza stagioni
di consolazioni pietrificate.
Undique, dunque, verso il battito finale
di nostra nuda natura.

E alle 10,45, davanti a un Provveditorato,
via del Risorgimento, Forlì,
che immagine mi dai dell'infinito?
Fine degli edita e munita templa serena
sapientum: non contenderemo più per dignità:
arrendiamoci al waiting for di questa Norchia
solare, neppure semota metu, ma pure per noi
così inevitabile, e dunque...
(le immagini tutte si leccano le penne dietro alle spalle).

of Norchia, dear doors of tau,
dear hearts of the chasms of the greening tuff,
dear chasms without seasons, without seasons
of petrified consolations.
From everywhere, therefore, onwards to the last throb
of our naked nature.

And at 10:45 AM, before the Superintendent's office,
via del Risorgimento, Forlì,
what image do you give me of the infinite?
Conclusion of the *lofty and safe peaceful temples
of the wise*:[16] we shall not contend anymore out of dignity:
let us surrender to the 'waiting for' of this solar
Norchia, not *even kept at length by fear*,[17] and yet
so inevitable for us, and therefore...
(all the images lick their feathers behind their backs).

E se, favoleggiando gli antichi
(non nate ancora le muse cui rivolgersi, non sorrise ancora le acque
d'oro della poesia delle isole delle grazie più circoscritte e felici)
cominciarono esseri a popolare
offuscati colli selve offuscate d'erbe e di foglie pinete fredde
erbe in profumo e di gonfie polle capelveneri nubilosi schiudenti
l'acqua; acqua in trasparenze verdi di nubi foglie e veli di palpebre
acquee, e vegetali, e gli insetti ancora leggeri tessenti il nido sotto.
E forniva l'equisetum i fusti suoi lunghi come adesso ai margini dei f
ma intere foreste d'equisetum giganteum danzavano alla luna, e l'equi
splendeva, lunghe raggiere di aghi silvestri fili rotanti d'equisetum sc
la splendente raggiera della luna.
Che evoluzioni i tuoi lunghi capelli vegetali, quali dinastie, capelvene
senza mai pensare ad unici dei, o pensando. Senza mai pensare a dio c
e dio alce, senza mai pensare agli dei animali delle nostre generazioni
Che generazioni equisetum. Che profumo di seta in ibridi verdi oscur
che grandi augusti fili verdi i tuoi rami, equisetum, di cui non mi sazi
di pronunciare il nome, perché, nella poesia, si sa, è poco, quel che res
a significare la meraviglia delle povere cose, per i poveri uomini

And if, when the ancients were telling tales
(not yet born the muses whom one addresses, not yet smiling the golden
waters of poetry of the islands of the most circumscribed and happy graces)
creatures began to inhabit
befogged hills, forests dimmed with grasses and leaves, cold pine forests,
grasses in perfume, cloudy maidenhairs spurting water of swollen
pools; water in green transparencies of clouds leaves and veils of watery
lids, and vegetables, and the yet weightless insects were weaving their
  [nests underneath.
And equisetums furnished their long stems like today at the edges of ditches
while whole forests of gigantic equisetums danced under the moon, and
  [equisetums
shone bright, long rays of wild needles, rotating equisetum threads under
the resplendent halo of the moon.
What evolutions, o maidenhair fern, your long vegetable hair, what
  [dynasties,
without ever thinking of single gods, or thinking. Without ever thinking
  [of deer-god
or elk-god, without ever thinking about the animal gods of our generations.
What generations, equisetum. What perfume of silk inside the hybrid dark
  [greens;
what large majestic green threads your branches, equisetum, whose name
I never tire to utter, because, in poetry, every one knows, little is left
to signify the wonder of poor things, for the poor men who,

che poveri, in ispirito, vogliano ancora, desiderare.
O dio che germini dalle acque; o dio, che quando giganti gli equisetu
fornivano foreste tranquille ondose, e gonfie e vaste, ammiccanti nel
alle future evoluzioni, dove il dio germinante delle acque scagliava
le cellule future di connubi presenti in equori senza più limiti,
prima degli uomini e prima degli uccelli, i vegetali che gridano in
connubi infiniti senza occhi né mai scossi d'onde di vento, in
gorgogli di mari e torrenti e cascate o ristagni d'acqua, sospinti
da mani virenti; brulicanti verdi su verdi; trasfiniscon le gemme
su gemme erboree d'umido contatto, in infiniti connubi
che tutti si seminano per i futuri indicibili.
Infiniti futuri di felci—dove le piume posero gli uccelli del sottobosco
Corimbi di piante che di nome non ebbero memoria negli anni lungh
dei cataloghi. Corimbi che quasi s'appropriarono fulgide foreste di
fauni. Corimbi che corsero saltando i fauni.
Corimbi che sui capi ancora indorati poserebbero fulgenti.
Corimbi. At nitidae surgunt fruges ramique virescunt
arboribus. E ancora negli anni lunghi senza animali, per herbas
si va il suo vento e l'umido e il secco spartisce le selve.
E gli arbusti salgono exorta repente e terra.
Dove troveranno le piante dei vasi, le piante quotidiane
di giardini senza orti, di orti incerti l'insorgenza del
concilio genitale, anche se manca la stagione, e la terra
non vivida nutre germogli di primavera? In terris primordia rerum
felici risero vegetali non sorti dal vomere dell'uomo.
E la natura rimangia e ridà ciò che nel corpo suo dissolvente
perisce. Quod nunc, aeterno quia constant semine quaeque,

poor in spirit, might still have longings.
O god germinating from the waters; o god, when gigantic equisetums
furnished tranquil, undulating forests, both swollen and vast, nodding in
[the wind
to future evolutions, where the god germinating from the waters hurled
the future cells of present unions on boundless seas,
before men and before birds, the vegetables screaming in
infinite unions without eyes without hands tossed by waves of wind, in
gurglings of seas and torrents and waterfalls or in stagnant waters, driven
by greening hands, greens crawling on greens, buds overran
grassy buds wet to the touch, in infinite unions,
sowing themselves for unutterable futures.
Infinite futures of ferns—where did the birds lay the feathers of the
[undergrowth?
Corymbs of plants whose names were forgotten in the long years
of the catalogues. Corymbs which almost took over bright forests
of fauns. Corymbs the running fauns leaped.
Corymbs that could still be set bright on golden heads.
Corymbs. *The bright crops sprout, and the branches grow green
upon the trees.*[1] And again in the long years without animals, the wind
moves through *grass*[2] dividing the wet from the dry in the forests.
And shrubs spring up *suddenly arisen from*[3] the earth.
Where will the potted plants, the everyday plants
of gardens without orchards, of stale orchards, find the onset of the
genital council, even if the season is wanting, and lifeless earth
feeds spring shoots? *The beginnings of things on earth*[4]
vegetables not born of man's plough laughed joyfully.
And nature consumes and returns what dies inside her dissolving
body. *Because now, instead, since all things grow gradually from an
[inexhaustible seed,*[5]

in eterno ritornano i corpi, e felci vegetali, e stelle vegetali,
che il cielo e l'erba si pasce, ritornano, in lumina vitae,
la natura generatim pabula praebens. Unde aether sidera pascit?
Attente, nelle notti e nei giorni di stagioni consumate,
presero stelle e felci sostanze e corpi. Attenti per pabula laeta
corpora deponunt, per riposare di riposi senza meridiane.
Corpora deponunt, e si genera la stirpe nuova degli esseri squamosi
e degli uccelli che rompono le cortine del cielo fremendo le ali.
E i lunghi fruscii, e i lunghi silenzi delle erbe ebbero nuovi
inganni.
E ancora attendevano i fauni. La stirpe umana, dalle menti
percosse dalla necessità, ancora, giaceva nei semi del creato.
E tanto attesero i fauni; e furono anche loro, dunque,
di seme vegetale, di stirpe arborea, pensati. E così, tra selve
che non muoiono mi piace morire: natura reficit;
nec ullam rem, infatti, gigni patitur nisi morte adiuta aliena.

The bodies return eternally, and the vegetable ferns, and the vegetable stars,
and grass, which heaven feeds on, return *to the lights of life,*[6]
*nature furnished food for them after their kind. From what
source does the sky feed the stars?*[7]

Watchful, in the nights and in the days of consumed seasons,
stars and ferns took substance and body. Watchful on *pleasant pastures
flocks lay themselves down,*[8] to sleep their sleep without sundials.
They lay themselves down,[9] and there came to life the new race of scaly
     [beings
and of birds whose quivering wings rend the curtains of heaven.
And the long rustlings, and the long silences of the grasses hid new
     [deceptions.
And the fauns were still waiting. The human race, their minds
smitten by necessity, was still lying inside the seeds of creation.
And the fauns waited so long; and therefore they too were
of vegetable seed, of arboreal stock. And thus, I wish to die among
     [deathless
forests: *nature creates one thing from another
and lets no thing be born indeed unless another one dies.*[10]

Questa immaginazione è dedicata agli anni delle ere vegetali, prima che gli animali e l'animale « uomo », popolassero il mondo.

Possiamo solo immaginarci i paesaggi che dovevano essere splendidi, per ciò che ci rimane dalla storia fossile, e dalle specie, evolute, di alcune piante.

Incuriosente e sollecitante, per me, è la vita evolutiva delle piante; la loro vita sensibile, la loro capacità di propagazione, di adattamento all'ambiente, la loro « creatività » nell'ambiente stesso, le loro percezioni del resto del mondo, gli accoppiamenti e le visioni sotto gli astri, i corpi di vita vegetale, le cellule che—chissà—schiudevano nuove possibilità di cambiamenti; il destino vario cui il mondo cellulare era destinato, dopo il « passaggio » delle piante, per gli animali. Immaginiamo dunque un mondo solo vegetale, di cui si sa qualcosa però d'una rivoluzionaria storia susseguente la fase iniziale, totalmente vegetale; descritta da libri importanti quali le varie teogonie, le cosmologie, la bibbia, ecc. immaginiamolo, e scagliamoci la nostra fantasia.

Infine, proviamo a riflettere su di un'analisi sensista: prendiamo al solito una voce illustre per varie ragioni, di cui privilegiamo quella poetica, e cioè la voce di Lucrezio: facciamola muovere come ci sentiamo, con tutte le inquietudini del nostro desiderio di vita, del nostro voler propagarci, dopo morte, come le piante e la natura: perciò la chiusa: « nec ullam rem, gigni patitur nisi morte adiuta aliena ». (Lucrezio, De rerum natura, L. I, vv. 146–264).

Tutto il brano del "De rerum natura", ripeto, va tenuto presente, e sentito, anche in ciò che non è citato, ma cui solo segretamente si allude, per ricostruire il senso della poesia.

Per i riferimenti mitici, si vada da Esiodo alle cosmologie orientali a quelle indiane, o anche ugro finne, da Vico, al Leopardi degli anni 1817–23 (sino alla poesia « Alla primavera, o delle favole antiche »).

This fantasy is dedicated to the years of the vegetable eras, before animals and before animal "man" inhabited the world. We can only imagine the splendid landscapes from what is left in the history of fossils and from the evolved species of some plants.

The evolutionary life of plants intrigues me and whets my curiosity: their sensitive life, their capacity for propagation, for adaptation to the environment, their "creativity" in a given environment, their perceptions of the rest of the world, the unions and visions under the stars, the bodies of vegetable life, the cells which—who knows?—opened new possibilities for change, the different fates to which the cellular world was destined after the "passage" of plants to the animal world. Let us imagine, therefore, a world that is only vegetable, of which something is known of a revolutionary history subsequent to the initial phase, totally vegetable. Let us imagine it as it is described in important books such as in the various theogonies and cosmologies, the Bible, etc. Let us imagine this and let us fling our imagination at its encounter.

Last, let us reflect on a sensist analysis: let us take as usual a famous voice, let us privilege, for various reasons, the poetic voice, the voice of Lucretius: let us make it move according to our feelings, with all our anxieties derived from our desire for life, from our wish to propagate ourselves, after death, like plants and nature. This is the reason for the ending: "*nec ullam rem, gigni patitur nisi morte adiuta aliena.*"* (Lucretius, *De rerum natura*, Vol. I, ll. 146–264).

All of this section of *De rerum natura* should be borne in mind and felt, even in what has not been quoted, but which is secretly alluded to, in order to rebuild the sense of the poetry.

As to the mythical references, they range from Hesiod to the oriental cosmologies, from the Indian cosmology to the Ugro-Finnish one, from Vico to Leopardi of the years 1817–23 (up to his poem "To Spring, or about Ancient Fables.").

---

* *nature creates one thing from another and lets no thing be born unless another dies.* (Copley and Treitel)

Notes

Bibliography of Latin Texts

Lucretius, *On the Nature of Things.* A new translation by Charles E. Bennett. New York: Walter J. Black, 1946.

Lucretius, *The Nature of Things: A new translation* by Frank O. Copley. New York: Norton, 1977.

Titi Lucreti Cari, *De rerum natura.* Edited and translated by Cyril Bailey. Oxford: The Clarendon Press, 1947.

Lucretius. *On the nature of the Universe.* Translated by Ronald Latham. Harmondsworth, Middlesex, England, Penguin Books; New York, New York, 1951.

Ovid, *Metamorphoses.* Translated by Rolfe Humphries. Bloomington: Indiana University Press, 1955.

Virgil. [Works English & Latin.] with an English translation by H. Rushton Fairclough. New and rev. ed. Cambridge, Mass., Harvard University Press; London, William Heinemann Ltd., 1935.

Virgil, *Eclogues.* Translated by Guy Lee. London: Penguin Classics, Penguin Books, 1984.

EPIGRAPH

1 ...*haec aëra rarum*
sufficiunt nobis et splendida lumina solis
Lucretius, DRN, II, 107-108. (Bailey, Copley, Latham, Notley)

THE REPOSE OF THE GREEN

1 from (Gk.), *hélios* [sun], and *chrysos* [gold], of the stonecrop family like seedum, life-forever or sempervivum, houseleek and others.

NARCISSUS

1 *àriston men ùdor,*
Pindar, Olympian 1, Vol. 1. (Copioli)
2 *arrides* (Notley)
3 Sic *attenuatus amore / liquitur et tecto paulatim carpitur igni—*
Ovid, M, p. 72, II, 487–89. (Notley and Humphries)

PENTHEUS

1 *Accessi sacris, Baccheaque sacra frequento*
Ovid, M, p. 79 II, 690–691. (Notley and Humphries)

DAPHNE

1 *Mollia cinguntur tenui praecordia libro,*
In frondem crines, in ramos brachia crescunt;
Pes modo tam velox pigris radicibus haeret—
Ovid, M, p. 19, II, 449–450. (Humphreys)
2 *praedam pedibus petit,*
Ibid., p. 19, I, 435.

FLORA

1 *Mansit odor,*
Ovid, Fasti, Book v, II, 375–76. (Notley)
2 *tenues secessit in auras.*
Ibid (Notley).
3 *posses scire fuisse deam—*
Ibid (Notley)

"Mossy springs, and grass softer than sleep,"

1. *Muscosi fontes et somno mollior herba,*
   et quae vos rara viridis tegit arbutus umbra,
   solstitium pecori defendite: iam venit aestas
   torrida, iam lento turgent in palmite gemmae.
   Vergil, E, VII, 45–48 (Fairclough, Latham)

2. *Et somno mollior herba*
   Ibid.

3. *rara viridis tegit arbutus umbra*
   Ibid.

4. *iam lento turgent in palmite gemmae*
   Ibid.

FOR VIRGIL

1. *et humi nascentia fraga*
   Virgil, E, III, 92. (Fairclough)

2. *silvestris raris sparsit labrusca racemis,*
   Ibid., v, 7. (Fairclough and Notley)

3. *adspice*
   Ibid., v, 6. (Notley)

4. *sive sub incertas zephyris motantibus umbras,*
   Ibid., v, 5. (Fairclough and Treitel)

5. *Lenta salix quantum pallenti cedit olivae,*
   puniceis humilis quantum saliunca rosetis...
   Ibid., v, 16. (Fairclough and Notley)

6. *Daphnis ego in silvis, hinc usque ad sidera notus...*
   Ibid., v, 43. (Fairclough and Notley)

7. *altis de montibus umbrae*
   Ibid., I, 83. (Fairclough)

Translator's note: Daphnis, son of Hermes, a Sicilian shepherd of the Golden age, not to be confused with Daphne.

GYPSOPHILA

1. Gypsophila: baby's breath.

2 *Primum aurora novo cum spargit lumine terras,*
   et variae volucres nemora avia pervolitantes
   aera per tenerum liquidis loca vocibus opplent,
   quam subito soleat sol ortus tempore tali
   convestire sua perfundens omnia luce,
   omnibus in promptu manifestumque esse videmus.
   Lucretius, DRN, II, 145–149. (Copley, Treitel, Copioli)

TO CAMPANA
   1 Dino Campana, Italian poet (1885–1932)

THE VEGETATIVE SOUL
   1 Aglaia (Splendor): one of the three Graces
   2 Euphrosine (Mirth): one of the three Graces

"You bow with such neat astonishment, and at"
   1 absinthe: wormwood

"I triumph over myself, I triumph, I sink"
   1 *His rebus dictis,*
   from common Latin usage. (Notley)

"Let us scan proof upon proof"
   1 (Homeric Greek) vocative form of *Thumas* [soul, spirit, courage] (Benedictson)

"The weather is fair, but not to quiver is an unravelling of all yesses "
   1 *ducis in longum amores*
   Virgil, E, IX, 56. (Notley, Copioli, Treitel)
   2 *silet aequor,*
   Ibid., IX, 57. (same)
   3 *silet nox*
   Virgil, G, I, 247. (same)
   4 *silet*
   Virgil, E, IX, 57 (Fairclough)

5   *Et nunc omne tibi stratum silet aequor, et omnes, adspice...*
    Ibid., (Fairclough, Notley, Copioli, Treitel)
6   *ventosi ceciderunt murmuris aurae.*
    Ibid., IX, 58. (Notley, Copioli, Treitel)

"Look, everything returns, even the signs on the wall,"
   1 *adspice* (Notley)
   2 *et sol crescentis decedens duplicat umbras*
      Virgil, E, II, 67. (Fairclough, Lee and Notley)
   3 of the stonecrop family like helichrysum, seedum, life-forever, houseleek and others. See above "The Repose of the Green."

"What groves, what glades held you, water"
   1 *Quae nemora aut qui vos saltus habuere puellae*
      Naides, indigno cum Gallus amore peribat
      Virgil, E, X, 9–10. (Fairclough)
   2 *(etiam flevere myricae, pinifer illum etiam*
      sola sub rupe jacentem)
      Ibid., X, 13–14. (Fairclough)
   3 *(Unde amor iste—tibi—quid, insanis, tua cura).*
      Ibid., X, 21. (Fairclough)
   4 *Extremum hunc, Arethusa, mihi concede laborem*
      Ibid., X, 1. (Fairclough and Notley)

"Like still lifes"
   1 *circumscrivere* (Notley)

"Again, whatever ourselves may touch in sightless"
   1 *Denique, nos ipsi caecis quaecumque tenebris,*
      tangimus...
      Lucretius, DRN, II, 745–747. (Bennett)
   2 *quod quoniam vinco / si tango*
      Ibid., II, 746–747 (Notley)
   3 *caecis quaecumque tenebris*
      Ibid., II, 745–747. (Bennett)

4 *fieri nunc esse docebo.*
   Ibid., 747–748. (Latham and Notley)
5 *quaecumque—nescis?*
   Ibid., 745. (Bennett and Notley)
6 *Invenias*
   (Notley)
7 *caecigeni, solis qui lumina numquam dispexere*
   Ibid., 740–741. (Campbell)
8 *rursum docebo*
   Ibid., 744. (Latham and Notley)

---

1 *"quod quoniam vinco, (si tango) fieri nunc esse docebo"*...
   Lucretius, DRN, II, 746–747 (Bennett, Notley)
2 *fieri nunc esse docebo.*
   Ibid., II, 746–747 (Bennett, Notley)
3 *that which is revealed in the universe:* (Treitel)

"You see concerning the power of imagination and"
 1 *Vides* (Notley)
 2 *adsuefactus sum* (Notley)

"Yellow, the soft curve of the yellow glass"
 1 *manibus*
   Virgil, A, VI, 883. (Notley)

---

1 *Give lilies with full hands*
   Virgil, Aeneid, VI, 883. (Notley)

SUAVIS TEMPESTAS
 1 *Sweet season* (Notley)
 2 Smyrna: famous city, chosen as an example of an illustrious past.
   Norchia: Etruscan necropolis built into precipitous cliffs of tuff. The entrance (or antichamber) to the cave, which is the actual tomb, displays a carved "T" (tau), a cross shape which

is one of the forms of a pre-Christian cosmic symbol of the infinite.

3 *statio* (Notley)
4 *suavis natura* (Notley)
5 *sufficiunt nobis et splendida lumina solis:*
   Lucretius, DRN, II, 107–108. (Bailey, Copley, Latham, Notley)
6 *per opaca domorum*
   Ibid., II, 115. (Notley and Bennett)
7 *sufficiunt*
   Ibid., II, 107. (Bennett)
8 porous limestone
9 *Splendida lumina solis*
   Ibid., II, 108. (Bailey)
10 *perennis* (Notley)
11 *tempestas* (Notley)
12 *statio perennis* (Notley)
13 *praesertim cum tempestas adridet et anni*
   tempora conspergunt viridantis floribus herbas.
   Lucretius, DRN, II, 32–33. (Notley and Copley)
14 *undique pervenimus* (Notley)
15 *undique*
   Ibid., II, 93 (Notley)
16 *edita munita templa serena sapientum*
   Ibid., II, 7–8. (Notley and Bennett)
17 *semota metu*
   Ibid., II, 19. (Notley)

"And if, when the ancients were telling tales"

1 *At nitidae surgunt fruges ramique virescunt*
   arboribus
   Lucretius, DRN, I, 252. (Bailey)
2 *herbas* (Notley)
3 *exorta repente*
   Lucretius, DRN, I, 186. (Bailey, Latham, Notley)

4   *In terris primordia rerum*
    Ibid., I, 220. (Bailey, Notley)
5   *Quod nunc, aeterno quia constant semine quaeque,*
    Ibid., I, 200 (Notley)
6   *in lumina vitae,*
    Ibid., I, 227. (Notley)
7   *generatim pabula praebens. Unde aether sidera pascit*
    Ibid., I, 229. (Bailey)
8   *pabula laeta corpora deponunt*
    Ibid., I, 257–258. (Notley and Copley)
9   *Corpora deponunt*
    Ibid.
10   *…natura reficit;*
    nec ullam rem, gigni patitur nisi morte adiuta aliena.
    Ibid., I, 264–265 (Copley and Treitel)

AUTHOR'S NOTE

Ferns and *equisetums* were prehistoric plants. Equisetums, or horsetails, make up the family of Equisetaceae. In prehistoric times, some of these plants grew to be large trees. Now only dwarf versions remain. The equisetum bears no flowers and is more closely related to ferns than to flowering plants. Horsetails reproduce themselves both by spores and by sex cells. The plant releases the spores which germinate in damp places and grow into tiny plants. These plants produce male and female sex cells that unite and develop into mature horsetails. Horsetails are very common in ditches along Italian country roads. The plants have a slightly rigid, tubular stem with dark rings from which the radial vegetable threads begin to move outward (hence, I speak of "haloes"). Their green is very pleasant. A bunch of these plants forms what looks like a forest of threads which move with the slightest motion of the wind.

Corymb is a form of inflorescence in which the flowers

form a flat-topped or convex cluster, the outermost flowers being the first to open.

Maidenhair: any fern of the genus Adiantum, the cultivated species, which have fine, glossy stalks and delicate, finely divided fronds.

ROSITA COPIOLI

Born in Riccione, in the province of Emilia-Romagna, Italy, in 1948, Rosita Copioli studied Humanities and received a degree in Aesthetics under the guidance of Professor Luciano Anceschi. From 1979 to 1989, she directed the literary journal *L'altro versante*, which hosted the most lively discussions and suggestions after the experimentalism of the 1960's. Ms. Copioli published two poetry collections: *Splendida lumina solis*, Forum 1979, Viareggio prize "first book," and *Furore delle rose*, Guanda 1988, Montale prize. She also published *I giardini dei popoli sotto le onde*, Guanda 1991, and *Il fuoco dell'Eden*, Tema Celeste 1992, works in prose. Ms. Copioli has written and published several essays: "Tradurre poesia", Paideia 1983; "Narrare", Theoria 1985; "Tradizioni della poesia italiana contemporanea", Theoria 1988. A W. B. Yeats scholar, Ms. Copioli has edited *Il crepuscolo celtico*, Theoria 1987, and the anthology of essays *Anima Mundi*, Guanda 1988. She is short story editor for the publication of W.B. Yeats' short stories with Guanda. She will soon publish a play, *Elena*, and a book of short stories, *La Tigre di Siva*.

Ms. Copioli is a member of the Italian Aesthetics Association (AISE). She collaborates in literary journals and in Italian and international journals of art and philosophy. She is also contributing editor to the art journal *Tema celeste*, and is on the editorial staff of *L'anello che non tiene*. She writes for the cultural page of daily newspapers (*Repubblica, Il Giornale, L'Avvenire*.)

THE SUN & MOON CLASSICS

PIERRE ALFERI [France]
Natural Gaits 95 (1-55713-231-3, $10.95)
The Familiar Path of the Fighting Fish [in preparation]

CLAES ANDERSSON [Finland]
What Became Words [in preparation]

DAVID ANTIN [USA]
Death in Venice: Three Novellas [in preparation]
Selected Poems: 1963–1973 10 (1-55713-058-2, $13.95)

ECE AYHAN [Turkey]
A Blind Cat Black AND *Orthodoxies* [in preparation]

DJUNA BARNES [USA]
Ann Portuguise [in preparation]
The Antiphon [in preparation]
At the Roots of the Stars: The Short Plays 53 (1-55713-160-0, $12.95)
Biography of Julie von Bartmann [in preparation]
The Book of Repulsive Women 59 (1-55713-173-2, $6.95)
Collected Stories [in preparation]
Interviews 86 (0-940650-37-1, $12.95)
New York 5 (0-940650-99-1, $12.95)
Smoke and Other Early Stories 2 (1-55713-014-0, $9.95)

CHARLES BERNSTEIN [USA]
Content's Dream: Essays 1975–1984 49 (0-940650-56-8, $14.95)
Dark City 48 (1-55713-162-7, $11.95)
Republics of Reality: 1975–1995 [in preparation]
Rough Trades 14 (1-55713-080-9, $10.95)

ANDRÉ DU BOUCHET [France]
The Indwelling [in preparation]
Today the Day [in preparation]
Where Heat Looms 87 (1-55713-238-0, $12.95)

LEE BREUER [USA]
A Dog's Life [in preparation]

ANDRÉ BRETON [France]
Arcanum 17 51 (1-55713-170-8, $12.95)
Earthlight 26 (1-55713-095-7, $12.95)

DAVID BROMIGE [b. England/Canada]
The Harbormaster of Hong Kong 32 (1-55713-027-2, $10.95)
My Poetry [in preparation]

OLIVIER CADIOT [France]
Art Poétique [in preparation]

PAUL CELAN [b. Bukovina/France]
Breathturn 74 (1-55713-218-6, $12.95)
Lightduress [in preparation]
Threadsuns [in preparation]

CLARK COOLIDGE [USA]
The Crystal Text 99 (1-55713-230-5, $11.95)
Own Face 39 (1-55713-120-1, $10.95)
The Rova Improvisations 34 (1-55713-149-X, $11.95)
Solution Passage: Poems 1978–1981 [in preparation]
This Time We Are One/City in Regard [in preparation]

ROSITA COPIOLI [Italy]
The Blazing Lights of the Sun 84 (1-55713-195-3, $11.95)

RENÉ CREVEL [France]
Are You Crazy? [in preparation]
Babylon [in preparation]
Difficult Death [in preparation]

MILO DE ANGELIS [Italy]
Finite Intuition: Selected Poetry and Prose 65 (1-55713-068-X, $11.95)

HENRI DELUY [France]
Carnal Love 121 (1-55713-272-0, $11.95)

RAY DIPALMA [USA]
The Advance on Messmer [in preparation]
Numbers and Tempers: Selected Early Poems 24
  (1-55713-099-X, $11.95)

HEIMITO VON DODERER [Austria]
The Demons 13 (1-55713-030-2, $29.95)
Every Man a Murderer 66 (1-55713-183-X, $14.95)
The Merovingians [in preparation]

JOSÉ DONOSO [Chile]
Hell Has No Limits 101 (1-55713-187-2, $10.95)

ARKADII DRAGOMOSCHENKO [Russia]
Description 9 (1-55713-075-2, $11.95)
Phosphor [in preparation]
Xenia 29 (1-55713-107-4, $12.95)

LARRY EIGNER [USA]
readiness / enough / depends / on [in preparation]

RAYMOND FEDERMAN [b. France/USA]
Smiles on Washington Square 60 (1-55713-181-3, $10.95)
The Twofold Vibration [in preparation]

RONALD FIRBANK [England]
Santal 58 (1-55713-174-0, $7.95)

DOMINIQUE FOURCADE [France]
Click-Rose [in preparation]
xbo 35 (1-55713-067-1, $9.95)

SIGMUND FREUD [Austria]
Delusion and Dream in Wilhelm Jensen's GRADIVA 38
  (1-55713-139-2, $11.95)

ARMAND GATTI [b. Monaco/France]
The 7 Possibilities for Train 713 Departing from Auschwitz
  [in preparation]

MAURICE GILLIAMS [Belgium/Flanders]
Elias, or The Struggle with the Nightingales 79 (1-55713-206-2, $12.95)
Winter in Antwerp [in preparation]

LILIANE GIRAUDON [France]
Fur 114 (1-55713-222-4, $12.95)
Pallaksch, Pallaksch 61 (1-55713-191-0, $12.95)

ALFREDO GIULIANI [Italy]
Ed. *I Novissimi: Poetry for the Sixties* 55
  (1-55713-137-6, $14.95)
Verse and Nonverse [in preparation]

TED GREENWALD [USA]
Going into School that Day [in preparation]
Licorice Chronicles [in preparation]

JEAN GRENIER [France]
Lyrical and Philosophical Essays [in preparation]

BARBARA GUEST [USA]
  Defensive Rapture 30 (1-55713-032-9, $11.95)
  Fair Realism 41 (1-55713-245-3, $10.95)
  Moscow Mansions [in preparation]
  Seeking Air [in preparation]
  Selected Poems [in preparation]

HERVÉ GUIBERT [France]
  Ghost Image 93 (1-55713-267-4, $13.95)

KNUT HAMSUN [Norway]
  Rosa [in preparation]
  Under the Autumn Star [in preparation]
  Victoria 69 (1-55713-177-5, $10.95)
  Wayfarers 88 (1-55713-211-9, $13.95)
  The Wanderer Plays on Muted Strings [in preparation]
  The Women at the Pump 115 (1-55713-244-5, $14.95)

MARIANNE HAUSER [b. Alsace-Lorraine/USA]
  The Long and the Short: Selected Stories [in preparation]
  Me & My Mom 36 (1-55713-175-9, $9.95)
  Prince Ishmael 4 (1-55713-039-6, $11.95)
  Shootout with Father [in preparation]

JOHN HAWKES [USA]
  The Owl AND *The Goose on the Grave* 67 (1-55713-194-5, $12.95)

LYN HEJINIAN [USA]
  The Cell 21 (1-55713-021-3, $11.95)
  The Cold of Poetry 42 (1-55713-063-9, $12.95)
  My Life 11 (1-55713-024-8, $9.95)
  Writing Is an Aid to Memory 141 (1-55713-27-1, $9.95)

EMMANUEL HOCQUARD [France]
  The Cape of Good Hope [in preparation]

FANNY HOWE [USA]
  The Deep North 15 (1-55713-105-8, $9.95)
  Nod [in preparation]
  Radical Love: A Trilogy [in preparation]
  Saving History 27 (1-55713-100-7, $12.95)

SUSAN HOWE [USA]
  The Europe of Trusts 7 (1-55713-009-4, $10.95)

LAURA (RIDING) JACKSON [USA]
Lives of Wives 71 (1-55713-182-1, $12.95)

HENRY JAMES [USA]
The Awkward Age [in preparation]
What Maisie Knew [in preparation]

LEN JENKIN [USA]
Dark Ride and Other Plays 22 (1-55713-073-6, $13.95)
Careless Love 54 (1-55713-168-6, $9.95)
Pilgrims of the Night: Five Plays [in preparation]

WILHELM JENSEN [Germany]
Gradiva 38 (1-55713-139-2, $13.95)

STEVE KATZ [USA]
Florry of Washington Heights [in preparation]
43 Fictions 18 (1-55713-069-8, $12.95)
Swanny's Ways [in preparation]
Wier & Pouce [in preparation]

ALEXEI KRUCHENYKH [Russia]
Suicide Circus: Selected Poems [in preparation]

THOMAS LA FARGE [USA]
Terror of Earth [in preparation]

VALERY LARBAUD [France]
Childish Things 19 (1-55713-119-8, $13.95)

MICHEL LEIRIS [France]
Operatics [in preparation]

OSMAN LINS [Brazil]
Nine, Novena 104 (1-55713-229-1, $12.95)

NATHANIEL MACKEY [USA]
Bedouin Hornbook [in preparation]

JACKSON MAC LOW [USA]
Barnesbook [in preparation]
From Pearl Harbor Day to FDR's Birthday 126
  (0-940650-19-3, $10.95)
Pieces O' Six 17 (1-55713-060-4, $11.95)
Two Plays [in preparation]

CLARENCE MAJOR [USA]
Painted Turtle: Woman with Guitar (1-55713-085-x, $11.95)

THOMAS MANN [Germany]
Six Early Stories [in preparation]

F. T. MARINETTI [Italy]
Let's Murder the Moonshine: Selected Writings 12
  (1-55713-101-5, $13.95)
The Untameables 28 (1-55713-044-7, $10.95)

HARRY MATHEWS [USA]
Selected Declarations of Dependence (1-55713-234-8, $10.95)

FRIEDRIKE MAYRÖCKER [Austria]
with each clouded peak [in preparation]

DOUGLAS MESSERLI [USA]
After [in preparation]
Ed. *50: A Celebration of Sun & Moon Classics* 50
  (1-55713-132-5, $13.95)
Ed. *50²: Another Celebration* [in preparation]
Ed. *From the Other Side of the Century: A New American
  Poetry 1960–1990* 47 (1-55713-131-7, $29.95)
Ed. [with Mac Wellman] *From the Other Side of the
  Century II: A New American Drama 1960–1995* [in preparation]
River to Rivet: A Poetic Trilogy [in preparation]

MARÍA NEGRONI [Argentina]
Cage Beneath the Cloth [in preparation]

GÉRARD DE NERVAL [France]
Aurelia [in preparation]

VALÈRE NOVARINA [France]
The Theater of the Ears [in preparation]

CHARLES NORTH [USA]
New and Selected Poems [in preparation]

MAGGIE O'SULLIVAN [England]
Palace of Reptiles [in preparation]

SERGEI PARADJANOV [Armenia]
Seven Visions [in preparation]

MURRAY POMERANCE [Canada]
Magia D'Amore [in preparation]

ANTONIO PORTA [Italy]
Metropolis [in preparation]

ANTHONY POWELL [England]
Afternoon Men [in preparation]
Agents and Patients [in preparation]
From a View to a Death [in preparation]
O, How the Wheel Becomes It! 76 (1-55713-221-6, $10.95)
Venusburg [in preparation]
What's Become of Waring [in preparation]

SEXTUS PROPERTIUS [Ancient Rome]
Charm 89 (1-55713-224-0, $11.95)

RAYMOND QUENEAU [France]
Children of Clay [in preparation]

CARL RAKOSI [USA]
Poems 1923–1941 64 (1-55713-185-6, $12.95)

TOM RAWORTH [England]
Eternal Sections 23 (1-55713-129-5, $9.95)

NORBERTO LUIS ROMERO [Spain]
The Arrival of Autumn in Constantinople [in preparation]

AMELIA ROSSELLI [Italy]
War Variations [in preparation]

JEROME ROTHENBERG [USA]
Gematria 45 (1-55713-097-3, $11.95)

SAPPHO [Ancient Greece]
The Poems of Sappho [in preparation]

SEVERO SARDUY [Cuba]
From Cuba with a Song 52 (1-55713-158-9, $10.95)

ALBERTO SAVINIO [Italy]
Selected Stories [in preparation]

LESLIE SCALAPINO [USA]
Defoe 46 (1-55713-163-5, $14.95)

ARTHUR SCHNITZLER [Austria]
  Dream Story 6 (1-55713-081-7, $11.95)
  Lieutenant Gustl 37 (1-55713-176-7, $9.95)

GILBERT SORRENTINO [USA]
  The Orangery 91 (1-55713-225-9, $10.95)

ADRIANO SPATOLA [Italy]
  Collected Poetry [in preparation]

THORVALD STEEN [Norway]
  Don Carlos [in preparation]

GERTRUDE STEIN [USA]
  How to Write 83 (1-55713-204-6, $12.95)
  Mrs. Reynolds 1 (1-55713-016-7, $13.95)
  Stanzas in Meditation 44 (1-55713-169-4, $11.95)
  Tender Buttons 8 (1-55713-093-0, $9.95)
  Three Lives [in preparation]
  To Do [in preparation]
  Winning His Way and Other Poems [in preparation]

GIUSEPPE STEINER [Italy]
  Drawn States of Mind 63 (1-55713-171-6, $8.95)

ROBERT STEINER [USA]
  Bathers [in preparation]
  The Catastrophe 134 (1-55713-233-x, $13.95 [paper], $26.95 [cloth])

JOHN STEPPLING [USA]
  Sea of Cortez and Other Plays [in preparation]

STIJN STREUVELS [Belgium/Flanders]
  The Flaxfield 3 (1-55713-050-7, $11.95)

ITALO SVEVO [Italy]
  As a Man Grows Older 25 (1-55713-128-7, $12.95)

JOHN TAGGART [USA]
  Crosses [in preparation]
  Loop 150 (1-55713-012-4, $11.95)

FIONA TEMPLETON [Scotland]
  Delirium of Dreams [in preparation]

SUSANA THÉNON [Argentina]
distancias / distances 40 (1-55713-153-8, $10.95)

JALAL TOUFIC [Lebanon]
Over-Sensitivity [in preparation]

TCHICAYA U TAM'SI [The Congo]
The Belly [in preparation]

PAUL VAN OSTAIJEN [Belgium/Flanders]
The First Book of Schmoll [in preparation]

CARL VAN VECHTEN [USA]
Parties 31 (1-55713-029-9, $13.95)
Peter Whiffle [in preparation]

TARJEI VESAAS [Norway]
The Great Cycle [in preparation]
The Ice Palace 16 (1-55713-094-9, $11.95)

KEITH WALDROP [USA]
The House Seen from Nowhere [in preparation]
Light While There Is Light: An American History 33
(1-55713-136-8, $13.95)

WENDY WALKER [USA]
The Sea-Rabbit or, The Artist of Life 57 (1-55713-001-9, $12.95)
The Secret Service 20 (1-55713-084-1, $13.95)
Stories Out of Omarie 58 (1-55713-172-4, $12.95)

ROBERT WALSER [Switzerland]
Jakob von Gunten [in preparation]

BARRETT WATTEN [USA]
Frame (1971-1991) [in preparation]

ARNOLD WEINSTEIN [USA]
Red Eye of Love [in preparation]

MAC WELLMAN [USA]
The Land Beyond the Forest: Dracula AND *Swoop* 112
(1-55713-228-3, $12.95)
The Land of Fog and Whistles: Selected Plays [in preparation]
Two Plays: A Murder of Crows AND *The Hyacinth Macaw* 62
(1-55713-197-X, $11.95)

JOHN WIENERS [USA]
The Journal of John Wieners / is to be called [in preparation]

ÉMILE ZOLA [France]
The Belly of Paris (1-55713-066-3, $14.95)

*

Individuals order from:
Sun & Moon Press
6026 Wilshire Boulevard
Los Angeles, California 90036
213-857-1115
www.sunmoon.com

Libraries and Bookstores in the United States and Canada
should order from:
Consortium Book Sales & Distribution
1045 Westgate Drive, Suite 90
Saint Paul, Minnesota 55114-1065
800-283-3572
FAX 612-221-0124

THE BLAZING LIGHTS OF THE SUN
Rosita Copioli

Translated from the Italian by Renata Treitel

A pupil of the noted Italian aesthetician Luciano Anceschi, Rosita Copioli studied aesthetics at the University of Bologna. Accordingly, Copioli is as comfortable with the classics as she is with contemporary literatures. And her poetry evinces this range of interests. Working from the idea of the "beautiful" going back to Lucretius' *De rerum natura*, the poet explores the myths of origin and concepts of the infinite. For Copioli the beginning of life was a female genesis, and her expression of cosmic order, therefore, reflects, as translator Renata Treitel expresses it, "female auto-erotic fantasies of generation without copulation."

Copioli's text gives physicality to the world of origins and growth: from the seemingly lifeless winter plant to the exuberance, vigor, and lusciousness of a nature which grows of its "own accord." Copioli has published two collections of poetry, was the editor of *L'altro versante*, a journal of poetry and criticism, and has published a volume of essays.

$11.95